"Mataeo...you kissed me."

"And you kissed me back—twice."

Finally, she met his gaze. "Then you understand why you staying over is... We can't."

He was on the bed then. His big frame crowded her, leaving no space for retreat. "We can do anything we damn well please."

"*You* can." She rested back on the headboard and shrugged. "*I* can't."

Mataeo averted his gaze, mulling over her words in silence while smoothing a hand across his soft hair. Finally, he raised one shoulder in a lazy shrug. "Well, then."

He was kissing her—again—and *again* she kissed him back. It was foolish to even think of resisting. What for? This was all she dreamed of. Still, she made a weak effort at doing so when he released her mouth to trail his lips down her neck and across her chest.

Books by AlTonya Washington

Kimani Romance

A Lover's Pretense
A Lover's Mask
Pride and Consequence
Rival's Desire
Hudsons Crossing
The Doctor's Private Visit
As Good as the First Time
Every Chance I Get
Private Melody
Pleasure After Hours

ALTONYA WASHINGTON

has been a published romance novelist for 6 years. Her novel *Finding Love Again* won an *RT Book Reviews* Reviewer's Choice Award for Best Multicultural Romance in 2004. She works as a senior library assistant and resides in North Carolina. In 2009, AlTonya—writing as T. Onyx—released her debut erotica titles *Truth In Sensuality* and *Ruler of Perfection*. In August 2009 she released her debut audio title *Another Love*. In August 2011 she released *Private Melody* with Kimani Books. Coming late 2011 will be the twelfth release in her popular Ramsey saga, *A Lover's Hate*.

PLEASURE
After
Hours

ALTONYA
WASHINGTON

KIMANI
ROMANCE

Smart, Savvy, Sweet—Carolina girls rule!

KIMANI PRESS™

ISBN-13: 978-0-373-86242-9

Recycling programs
for this product may
not exist in your area.

PLEASURE AFTER HOURS

Copyright © 2012 by AlTonya Washington

www.kimanipress.com

Printed in U.S.A.

Dear Reader,

Pleasure After Hours warms my heart for many reasons. Temple Grahame is my first Carolina heroine. It was a refreshing experience to craft a character whose background held aspects that were so similar to my own. Another similarity was Temple's mother, Aileen Grahame. Aileen was my grandmother's name, and having the chance to bring part of her into the story made the writing that much sweeter.

Of course I can't forget Mataeo North. It would be a terrible understatement to describe him as simply sexy. He's as incredible inside the pages of this novel as he appears on the cover. I was motivated by the idea of a story between two characters who experienced closeness in all areas of their lives yet remained unattached in any romantic capacity. Bringing Mataeo and Temple together was definitely a provocative journey. Tell me what you think of it. Email me, altonya@lovealtonya.com.

Love,

AlTonya

Chapter 1

"Claude, what *is* this? I thought you were in love with me?"

A purely girlish laugh escaped Claudia Aspen's lips. Her vivid blue gaze sparkled wickedly as it was directed toward the honey-toned giant who studied her with a consciously seductive gaze.

"I swear this is business and not…personal, Mataeo."

"Hmph." Mataeo North's responding grunt held a playful undercurrent and he shook his head at the stunning sixty-something woman seated on the sofa opposite him.

"I swear it," Claudia persisted in a tone that was just as breathy as it was sensual. "Many of the clients feel the same as I do."

"Are we about to have problems, Claudia?"

"Why no, dear." Claudia half turned toward the tall, lovely, coffee-complexioned woman seated to her left. "I'm only here to open the floor for discussion."

"You mean to warn us." Temple Grahame smiled knowingly while Claudia patted her knee.

"Honey, no." Claudia gave a saucy toss of her frosted wheat-colored bob. "Mateo runs a first-class operation. You both do incredible work." She gave Temple's knee one final pat and then settled back to her side of the sofa. "It's just good business to let the clients know they're appreciated."

"By renegotiating already competitive rates?" Temple queried.

"By...patting our backs a little." Claudia recrossed her legs and smiled at Mateo.

He wasn't humored. "North Shipping's a private company, Claude, and it stays that way."

"Calm down, darlin'. Everyone knows you have no intention of going public, but many of the clients *would* be open to discussing current rates—in this economy that's fair to at least entertain, isn't it?"

A muscle flexed along Mateo's square jawline. Propping a fist to his cheek, he looked toward Temple.

"Well, Claudia, it appears that we're on the same wavelength." Temple waited for the woman to turn to her again. "Mateo and I have been working to put together a client weekend to begin with a dinner and round out with a series of individualized meetings to review the higher-end shipping agreements."

Claudia's mouth was in the shape of a perfectly glossy red O. "Why, Temple, that's...that's a marvelous idea." Her tone sounded more awed than sensual then. "Is this a secret or may I—"

"Oh, no, feel free to discuss it," Temple said, knowing Claudia would waste no time doing so regardless. "We haven't gotten all the particulars in place yet so it'll be several months into the future."

"Sweetheart, I certainly understand." Claudia leaned over to pat Temple's knee again. "This is a huge deal and will take quite a while to prepare. The mere promise of it will be great news for the clients. Oh—" She paused to retrieve her vibrating cell phone from the sofa cushion. "Excuse me, darlins. I need to take this."

Temple's hazel gaze locked with Mataeo's chocolate one and they headed to the other side of the office to give Claudia a measure of privacy.

"Client weekend?" He whispered when they stood near the floor-to-ceiling windows along the wall behind his desk. "Nice," he added.

"Thanks." Temple shrugged and glanced toward Claudia.

"So how much planning have you done?" He leaned against a window and settled both hands into his blue-gray trouser pockets.

"None." She joined in when he chuckled. "Just came up with it to pacify her." She tapped a rounded nail to her chin and appeared thoughtful. "But it *is* a good idea. Don't know when I'd have time to plan something that extravagant, though."

"Thanks, anyway." Mataeo took her hand and tugged until she leaned close for the kiss he placed on her jaw.

She patted his cheek. "My job, remember?"

"No, really, Temp. Thanks." He squeezed her hand

as his warm, deep stare shifted in Claudia's direction. "She's been a lot harder to take lately."

"Taeo..." Temple's entrancing eyes narrowed in suspicion. "You haven't slept with her, have you?"

Grinning, Mateo laid Temple's hand against his chest. "No. I swear it," he added when her brow arched a notch higher. He winced a little. "I swear I've never slept with her. Just don't ask me to take any more meetings at her lake house."

Temple laughed.

"Damn." Mateo checked the inside jacket of his suit coat. "Now *I'm* vibrating."

The timing was perfect. Claudia Aspen had finished her call and was avidly observing the couple near the window.

"You two look lovely together," she mentioned when Temple approached.

"Claudia...we work together, that's all."

"I'm sure it is, honey." Claudia kept her eyes on Mateo while he handled his call. "I don't think I'd be quite as professional working under—I mean *with* that."

Temple rolled her eyes. "Claudia, has anyone ever told you that you're too much?"

"A time or two." Claudia shrugged as if it were of little consequence to her. "But even *you* can't deny *that* is too much man to go...untested."

"Well, you help yourself." Temple bent to grab Claudia's portfolio. "I'm afraid you'd be among the masses." She handed Claudia the leather-bound book. "*That* is not a one-woman man."

Claudia shrugged, tucked the portfolio beneath her

arm and squeezed Temple's elbow. "Well, darlin', that depends on who the woman is, now doesn't it?"

Temple set both hands on her hips. She watched as Claudia blew a kiss toward Mataeo and then sashayed out of the room.

"Would you *please?*"

Temple knew her below-the-breath hiss would do nothing to still the man who stood before her. A full-blown bellow would do nothing to encourage cooperation, either, she was sure. As usual, her boss had requested her "assistance" while he did nothing to *assist.*

"Dammit, Nev." Mataeo's sandpaper tone surged and his grip tightened on the phone receiver. "Forget it, I'll handle it. Forget it, Nevil."

Temple leaned back where she sat on the edge of the desk when Mataeo moved close to slam the cordless back to the mount.

"So what am I handling?" she asked after his breathing had filled the office with sound for more than five seconds.

"What?" His response held an absent tinge.

Temple's long, light gaze softened with a mix of humor and mild agitation. "Whenever I hear you tell someone that *you'll* handle it that means *I'll* handle it."

"Ah, Temp." The easy charm Mataeo seemed to possess in droves came through for him then. "You know you're so much better at most things than I am."

Unfortunately, the charming effort fell short of his right hand. Right *arm* seemed a more fitting description.

"Just cut it out and tell me what I'm taking care of

this time." Temple returned her focus to the silver-gray tie she was securing about Mataeo's neck.

The fact that Mataeo North had no actual assistant was as amusing as it was intriguing. The man was notorious for going to Temple for everything from help with his tie to advice on whether the next deal was worth the pursuit. Any assistant hired for the shipping magnate was of little use. Eventually, the position was phased out entirely.

"Hold still." Temple slapped his forearm. "Unless you'd like to be choked, and I promise you, I can arrange it." She tugged the silver tie threateningly. "So what were you talking to Nevil about?" She frowned as she focused on securing the knot.

"Development was supposed to be in charge of planning the lion's share of the survey expedition for the new building site near the docks."

"Hmph." Temple's hands slowed over the knot she was making in the tie. "I didn't realize you'd already had a place in mind considering…" She dismissed the thought and continued with her task.

Mataeo's long brows drew close. "Considering what? That I haven't closed the deal yet?"

Temple merely shrugged.

"That's why I didn't tell you."

She smiled, feeling the smoky heat of his mocha stare boring into her. She could tell by the strain of the tie around his neck that his temper was on the rise.

"It's just that you've got some serious competition on this one." Her hands stilled again. "Sanford Norman wants Manson Yates's client list as badly as you do."

"Hell, Temp, *every* exporter along the Eastern Seaboard wants Manson Yates's client list. Sadly, many aren't in a position to accept his conditions for sale."

"And too bad for you Sanford Norman has his headquarters right here in good old Wilmington, N.C." Once again, Temple resumed her work on the tie.

Mataeo leaned down a bit to look into Temple's lovely coffee-brown face. "And that's the *only* hitch standing in the way of my closing this thing—a pretty pitiful hitch if you ask me."

Temple tapped his chin, instructing him to straighten. "From the reports I've read, that's enough. Thank you, Jesus," she whispered upon finishing with the tie. She knocked her fists against his broad chest to urge him out of the way.

Mataeo didn't move. "Do you think Sanford Norman's willing to set up new digs right on the dock to accommodate Manson Yates's clients *and* treat them in the manner they're accustomed to?"

Temple braced her hands along the desk, the natural arch of her brows rose as her suspicion set in. "I still don't know how you managed to convince…anyone to part with property in that area."

"Impressed?" Mataeo stood back and folded his arms across his chest. The glint in his rich chocolaty gaze dared her to deny that she was.

"Only if you close the deal." Temple made a pretense at quickly straightening the knot in his tie. "Otherwise you're just an idiot who paid too much for a piece of property he can't use."

"Why the hell do I keep you?" Mataeo went around his desk in search of his cell phone and keys. "You're no good for my ego."

"Which is considerable." Temple toyed with the box pleats at the hem of her tan skirt. "Lucky for you, you've got enough volunteers around to…stroke it."

Mataeo rose to his full six feet eight inches. "Funny." He tucked the phone into the jacket of his gray three-piece.

"But true." Temple didn't look away from her pleats. "You only keep me around to tie your ties."

"And a damn good job you do of it, too." He went back to searching his desk. A scowl shadowed his face as he massaged a hand across the back of his neck. "Temp, have you seen—"

The jingle of keys caught his ears and Mataeo looked up to see them dangling from Temple's fingers.

"I keep you around for everything that matters." He shook his head and grimaced while voicing the confession. He leaned across the desk. "You know I can't function without you."

Temple laughed and brushed a playful slap to his flawless cheek. "You'd be just fine."

"You're wrong. I need you for everything that matters." His stare didn't waver. "Like this lunch."

"Taeo…" She rolled her eyes. "Don't start, not about this. You know how I feel about us taking on more clients right now." She watched him with accusation lurking in her hazel eyes. "This is all about your greed and that damn win-at-all-costs competitive streak of yours."

"That's what business is all about, Temp." He moved from behind the desk.

"That may be, but it's getting more dramatic every day, and I've had enough."

Mataeo's glare harbored more concern than anger.

Temple shifted her gaze back to the hem of her skirt. Silently, she cursed her slipup as she noticed the uncertainty creeping onto Mataeo's handsome face.

"I just prefer playing this one from the background, you know?"

Soothed by her fast clarification, Mataeo gave a slow nod.

Temple leaned over and tugged his jacket lapel as if to set it straight. "You should get going unless you want Sanford Norman entertaining Mr. Yates over drinks while they wait for you."

"Right." Mataeo grimaced and pushed himself from the desk. "I'll see you later. You're heading home, right?"

It wasn't exactly a question. He knew his right arm/ best friend well enough to know her routine rarely changed unless *he* changed it.

He stopped just before the double doors to his office suite and turned to ply her with a crooked smile. "Last chance for lunch? My treat?"

Temple blew him a kiss. "Good luck."

North Shipping may have been one of the many exporting businesses along the Eastern Seaboard but few compared to the savvy of its owner and the success he'd garnered in the field. Much of that had to do with the crew of employees Mataeo surrounded himself with. Everyone was at the top of their game from the entry-level shipping clerks to the man's righthand/right arm, Temple Grahame.

The fact that they were friends—the best of friends, for many years—was an added perk in an already powerful relationship. Taeo and Temp, as they were known by most of their business associates, seemed to complement each other in every situation, be it professional or personal.

Of course, everyone speculated that they were more than friends. This was no surprise considering Mataeo North was both idolized and envied by most men he knew. This fact had as much to do with his business prowess as it had to do with his sexual conquests.

With that in mind, a woman like Temple Grahame wouldn't spend her days in his sights and remain unnoticed for long. Especially when her looks—as well as her personality—were enough to literally stop a man. With her wide, hazel stare and soft hypnotic voice, Temple struck most as delicate, understated and nonconfrontational. She was, without a doubt, the polar opposite of her boss.

Temple Grahame, however, was no floor mat. That truth was simply one of the millions of reasons Mataeo North trusted her with his life and livelihood.

Sequestered in the mellow environment of her office, Temple wouldn't let herself dwell on how her leaving would affect him. Thankfully, there was a knock on her door that set aside the troubling thoughts that were rising. She left her desk when she saw Megaleen Barnum poke her head inside the room.

"This a good time?" Megaleen called out with a wave and a smile.

"Perfect time," Temple greeted her attorney with a hug.

"So how goes the head-hunting?" Megaleen set her things on the cream suede sofa near the door.

"I think I've pretty much narrowed it down." Temple sounded upbeat. "Taeo's gonna need quite a few people in here to handle everything he's got me covering."

"Including screening calls from jilted lovers?"

"Shh…" Temple scolded her friend playfully. "There're some things he's gonna have to learn to handle on his own."

"So are you sure he'll let you go just like that when you tell him what you have in mind?" Meg asked once their laughter had softened.

"I don't see why not." Temple propped one hand on her hip and massaged her neck with the other. "People resign positions every day, don't they?"

"Yeah." Meg strolled the office with hands propped on her hips, as well. "But there *is* the potential for drama and speculation when the one resigning is second in command for a multinational shipping corporation." Meg turned to face her client with a curious light blue stare. "Do you really think it'll be a stress-free event?"

"Oh, Meg." Temple massaged her neck with both hands then. "I don't expect it to be blissful, but it won't be overwhelming. I'm putting a lot of good people in place here." Her voice held the slightest twinge of doubt.

Meg heard it clearly. "Mataeo won't be the only one with questions, you know?" She smoothed her black pin-striped skirt and took one of the chairs in front of Temple's desk. "The first thing people will think is that there are business woes and that you're getting out while the gettin's good."

Temple smirked and took her place along an over-extended windowsill. "No, Meg, the first thing people will think is that we had some kind of lover's spat and that I'm leaving him over it."

Megaleen focused on her twiddling thumbs and didn't reply. It went without saying that her client/friend had taken the unfair brunt of the negative aspects to being the right arm of one of the most powerful men in the shipping world.

Mataeo North had garnered money, success and adoration—sexual *and* scholarly. Temple, meanwhile, had dealt with the rumors, name-calling and doubts over whether she was truly qualified to hold such a weighty post.

As if she could have done anything about it had she tried. Looking the way she did, the assumption was that she'd reached such lofty heights working from the bedroom or wherever Mataeo North desired to have her. The woman was far too lovely to have made her way in the world by using her brain of all things.

Megaleen had heard it too often in the circles she ran in as a business attorney. Most of the women Mataeo employed hated her friend with a passion. Their reasons had little to do with the intellect and business savvy Temple possessed, but with the coffee-brown complexion that needed no enhancements. Meg doubted the woman owned a lick of foundation. Then there was the healthy bust and bottom size, model-quality legs and the almost nonexistent waistline which set the envy a step further.

"He'll understand why I need to do this." Temple's soft voice sounded even fainter as she studied the view of Wilmington's city streets below. "As long as we keep our friendship intact—that's the most important thing."

Meg smothered a sigh while flipping a lock of auburn hair between her fingers. Temple Grahame's greatest asset was her kindness and she paid dearly for it. She truly believed that decency and treating others fairly would ensure the same treatment in return. Oh, boy, didn't she believe that about Mataeo North, Meg mused.

Pushing out of the chair, Megaleen headed for the coffee table while praying Temple never had to find out otherwise. She took the portfolio from the table and gave it a wave.

"Should we go over this before either of us gets called away?"

Roaring laughter from the table of five men drew hardly any attention—most of the tables inside the G-Red Gallery were filled with laughing men. The place was a popular lunch destination specializing in steak, seafood and beer created in-house by the establishment's own brewery.

Manson Yates's happy bellow, though, could easily rival any of the other male patrons' in the place.

"Good thinkin', San, for suggesting this place!" Manson clapped Sanford Norman's shoulder. "I don't travel down to G-Red nearly as much as I used to."

"You're welcome, Mr. Yates." Sanford attempted a humble nod while sending a cunning wink in Mataeo's direction.

Unfazed, Mataeo tilted his beer mug in a mock toast.

"Does business keep you away, sir?" he asked Manson Yates.

The older man chuckled. "Hell no, this place is perfect for business! No, son, my reason is far more demanding than business—it's my wife!"

More wild laughter resumed. Even the waiter, who'd arrived to hear Manson's explanation, submitted to his own share of grinning.

"A nag of a wife'll do it every time!" Sanford railed after tossing back what remained of his beer. "I swear some of my best wet dreams have been ruined by the sound of Regina's voice in my subconscious!"

The laughter following that was noticeably less boisterous, primarily because Manson Yates didn't appear amused.

"I adore my wife, San," the man confirmed, a stern expression sharpening his weathered features. "Her *nagging* me not to come here has more to do with my doctor's instructions that I stay off red meat, and since G-Red has the best and biggest cuts around…"

"Apologies, sir." Sanford gave a quick, phony cough while pressing a fist to his mouth. "I meant no disrespect. Your wife's a beautiful woman."

"Yes, she is, and you should treasure *yours*." Manson tilted his beer bottle in Sanford's direction. "A wife is a man's most trusted supporter, but only if she's treated properly."

Sanford nodded, but there was no agreement dwelling in his hooded green stare.

"You don't look convinced, San." Mataeo decided to call him on it.

Again, Sanford cleared his throat. "That's not it." He waved toward the waiter for a refill.

"What is it then?" Manson inquired.

Sanford ran a finger along the inside of his collar. "Just not all of us have been as lucky as you to find a woman like the one you've been blessed to marry." He tapped his index and middle finger to his forehead and offered Mataeo a mock salute. "You're smart to hold on to your freedom, man."

"Nonsense." Manson was shaking his head. "Don't listen to it, kid. There's nothin' like building a life with a woman you love, trust and desire," he told Mataeo before turning back toward Sanford. "If you view your marriage as less than a blessing, perhaps you should consider improving your role as a husband."

Manson didn't wait for Sanford's response but turned his focus back to Mataeo. "There anyone special, son?" he asked and shot Sanford a glare when the man chuckled over the question.

Mataeo shrugged, finding no cause to be less than honest. "There're actually *several* special someones."

"Ha!" Manson dragged a hand through a shock of white hair. "Nonsense—no such thing. There can only be one," he declared with a wink and a smirk.

"Business can be sweet when it's successful but it can be a cold bitch on most nights." Manson paused to take a swig from the fresh, chilled bottle the waiter set before him. "Love, marriage and family are what keep a man sane and keep him in the game." He downed a healthy swig and then waved at someone across the sunlit dining room. "Fellas, I see a friend I should speak to."

"Don't let the old man fool you," Sanford cautioned Mataeo when they were the only two at the table. "When it comes down to passing along that client list of his, it's gonna be about who has the better cold bitch of business—not the better wife or…special someones."

Mataeo supplied a cool smile and barely raised a brow. He and Sanford enjoyed their drinks in silence until Manson Yates returned.

Chapter 2

"Are we still headed for Ms. Grahame's, boss?"

"Yeah," Mataeo mumbled raggedly as he made his way into the Maybach following his nerve-trying lunch with Manson Yates and Sanford Norman.

Feeling edgy regarding the close of a business deal wasn't a thing he experienced regularly. In truth, it wasn't the deal that had him on edge. He'd be damned if he could understand why marriage, or the lack thereof, would get to him when it never had and when he'd doubted it ever would.

Yet there he sat in the back of a ridiculously expensive car, bought and paid for with his own sweat and blood, and pondered his worth as a man.

Special someones were things most often taken lightly. Still, they came in quite handy on the nights when the "cold bitch" of business was kicking his butt.

So why had he done his damnedest to avoid them

for the better part of the past five months? Had it been longer? Was he disillusioned? Did he need to freshen up his stock? Were Manson Yates's words truer than he cared to admit?

"Crap," he muttered, having whipped open the bar to discover his favorite whiskey was running dangerously low.

"Ro?"

"Yeah, boss?" Roland Sharp called from the front of the car.

"We need to restock the bar back here."

"I'm on it, boss."

Mataeo drained the last from the blocky bottle. He settled back against the comfortably cool leather seats while musing that his drink was one "special someone" that never disappointed. He closed his eyes and let his mind go blank for a time.

Perhaps he really did need to just freshen up his stock, he resolved upon opening his eyes. The current lineup, while beautiful and seriously eager to please, had fallen into the same mode of behavior as so many others who had come his way in the past.

Despite knowing they weren't the only ones who warmed his bed, each fancied herself the one who would give him cause to abandon his freedom. Then what Sanford Norman referred to as "nagging" began. It never failed to intrigue Mataeo how rigorously a woman could "nag" when the possibility of commitment loomed far off into the horizon. This behavior ran the spectrum from the most freaky and promiscuous to the most intelligent and reserved.

Replenishing the stock wouldn't be a problem at all

for Mataeo. Not when his physical gifts were so dangerously appealing. Even women already schooled on his
success with the opposite sex were unfailingly lured to
the provocative flame he generated. His massive build
was just shy of 6 foot 8 inches, which made it easy for
him to command attention the second he arrived in a
room. The honey-toned skin was as flawless as the taut
muscles it covered. A deep-set smoky brown stare was
fringed with shamefully long lashes; they even had the
nerve to curl at the ends. Such was also the case for
the curve of the mouth, equally as seductive and made
more sensual by the striking dimple in his chin.

Yes, the assets were many and erotically powerful.
Refreshing the stock wouldn't be a difficult or boring
chore. So why did he cringe at the thought of it? Roland's voice mixed into his thoughts.

"We've arrived at Ms. Grahame's, boss."

"I got the door, Ro." Mataeo had answered his own
question before he stepped onto the sidewalk outside
the condo tower. Replenishing the stock made him
cringe because somewhere along the way he'd lost complete and utter interest in it.

"You're early." Temple glanced at the wall clock in
her living room when she opened her front door.

"Told you I'd see you after lunch." Mataeo brushed
past her on his way inside.

It didn't take much more to clue Temple in to his
sour mood. She tossed her coarse, wavy hair, loosened
from its usual confines of a chignon or coiled braid,
and took note of the stiffness in Mataeo's wide back.

"Well, I'm taking a call in the back so…grab a drink or something."

"What do you think I'm on my way to do, Temp?"

Temple rolled her eyes and waved him off as she headed back to her home office.

"Damn." Mataeo figured it just wasn't his night, having opened the cabinet to the bar to find the Jim Beam running dangerously low there, as well. Shaking his head, he poured what remained into a stout glass and dialed the car from his phone.

"Ro? Grab an extra bottle of Beam for Ms. Grahame, will you?" With a quarter-filled glass in hand, Mataeo strolled into the living room.

In spite of his frightful mood, he couldn't help but smile as he often did whenever he spent time at Temple's place.

If the term "old school" ever fit anyone, it was Temple Grahame, he thought. The second oldest in a huge Southern family, her old-fashioned nature was a thing one could almost see.

Mataeo passed the sound system that, while state of the art, didn't garner half as much use as the record player Temple had inherited from an aunt, who also left her prized possession of classic soul vinyls.

Mataeo studied the back of an album cover, nodding to the beat of the Curtis Mayfield piece that filled the room with its slick melody. Laughter in the distance caught his ear below the rhythm. Mataeo set down the cover, emptied his glass and headed toward the sounds.

Temple sat on the edge of her desk with her back to the door. With her bare feet propped on the seat of her chair, she faced a gorgeous view of late-afternoon

Wilmington. As the sun set, the skyline gradually illuminated, offering a more brilliant picture of the city.

Mataeo smiled, enjoying the lazy drawl of her voice while she chatted. He wasn't so much focused on her words as he was on the manner in which they were delivered. How many times had that voice alone soothed raging tempers during heated business conferences? He absently fiddled with his vest pocket as he thought it over.

Temple laughed again, catching Mataeo's full attention. That time he was quite interested in the words she spoke, especially when he heard the name *Kendall*.

"Well, we'll just see if you're still talking so bold when I see you in a few weeks…ha! Right. Thanks Kendall…mmm-hmm… See you soon."

Temple smiled, studying the cordless until Mataeo cleared his throat and grabbed her attention. "Damn you, Taeo." She clutched her chest when she saw him in the doorway.

Mataeo barely managed to smile as she whirled around on the desk and faced him. Though she never raised her voice, her curses held a definite sting when they were directed his way.

"You taking a trip?" He ignored her agitation.

Temple eased off the desk. "That was Kendall Ingram. He's a Realtor helping Mama settle some business on a property."

Mataeo straightened from his leaning stance against the doorjamb. Obvious concern sharpened his already striking features. "Does Miss Aileen need help with anything?"

Waving off the gesture, Temple walked around her

desk. "Everything's fine—nothing to worry about. So why don't you spend your time telling me about that lunch meeting instead?"

Though he grimaced, Mataeo didn't seem to notice her subject change. "We were done talkin' business before we ordered the first drink."

"God, *that* bad?" Temple gathered the hem of her ankle-length peach housedress.

Focused on business once more, Mataeo moved to let her pass. He followed her from the office and back toward the kitchen.

"Depends on which conversation you're referring to—business or the other." He doffed his suit coat and dropped it on the back of an armchair. "The other got pretty weird," he added.

"Weird?" A smile curved Temple's generous mouth. "I wouldn't associate that word with a man like Manson Yates."

"Hmph. You would if you tossed Sanford Norman into the mix."

"Ah…" Temple was browsing her cabinet. "What'd he say or do this time?" Gradually, Temple lost interest in her soup hunt as Mataeo explained the lunch topic.

"Weird indeed…." She turned back to the cabinet. "Then again, Manson Yates *has* been married almost fifty years. He and his wife have been together since they were teenagers."

"Keeping up with the society pages, huh?" Mataeo's gravelly voice softened on the question.

She gave a toss of her head and an awkward shrug. "Strong marriages are rare. When you hear about one, you pay attention."

Mateo wasn't sure how to respond, so he went to search the refrigerator. "Well, the man's dead serious when it comes to holy matrimony." He studied the selection of juices along the door. "Didn't mind telling me what he thought of *my* love life, that's for damn sure."

"Really?" Amusement crept into Temple's light eyes. "And what does he think about it?" She set about heating up a large can of chicken tortilla soup.

Mateo decided on what to drink while muttering something foul. "It's just obvious that man's got a thing for commitment and vows and whatever the hell else goes along with it."

"Mateo…" Temple set the pot to simmer and then turned to him. Disbelief had replaced her amusement. "Tell me you're not thinking that Yates might base his decision on whether you're married or not."

It was Mateo's turn to shrug awkwardly. "I don't think I have to be married." He chugged down a bit of the pineapple juice. "But he made it clear that he didn't approve of me dancin' from one pair of arms to the next." He slanted her a wink.

Temple lowered the heat under the soup. "Well, I hope he doesn't think Sanford's any more noble."

"Is that right?" Mateo drew closer, intrigued and not at all ashamed by wanting in on a bit of gossip. "You know somethin'?"

"Not much." Temple reached for a soup mug that was hanging along the wall near the microwave. "One of his assistants goes to the same hair salon as me. Word is, any day they're expecting the Normans to announce a divorce."

"Mmm-hmm." Mateo pondered the information

while taking a swig of the juice. At the same time, he reached behind Temple for the remote to the TV above her wine rack.

Temple rolled her eyes. "What's the *mmm-hmm* about?" She stirred the hearty soup.

"Just sounds like we're on even ground, after all."

"Ha! I honestly don't know whether to laugh or cry over how well I can read you."

Mataeo only chuckled while surfing the channels.

"Please tell me you're not gonna try fooling Yates into believing that you've seen the error of your ways and are now ready for a serious relationship?"

"Jesus, Temp." He looked away from the TV and fixed her with a look of outraged innocence. "Not that I'd ever do something so low—" he ignored her knowing glare "—but I wouldn't even have to go that far. Sanford put his foot in his mouth revealing so much about his own marriage I think he lost a few points with Yates."

"This isn't a popularity contest, Taeo," Temple sang while heading to the refrigerator for cheese. "It's about whose got the better business for Manson Yates's clientele."

"You know, it doesn't help that you sound an awful lot like Norman right about now." Mataeo leaned against the counter and focused on the television again.

"Well, at least one of you is thinking." Temple headed over to lace the bubbling soup with shredded Colby cheese.

"I never forget that, Temp. My guess is that Norman knows who has the better business. I could see it in his eyes when he said it."

Temple shook her head in response to Mateo's confidence, but offered no comment. She turned the heat down to low and rubbed her hand across his chest when she passed on her way out of the kitchen.

"Congratulations," she said.

"Not so fast." Mateo shut off the TV and followed her to the living room. "I still want you to go with me to this cocktail party."

"You say this like I know what you're talking about." Frown lines marred Temple's brow. "What cocktail party?"

"Party and dinner. Yates and his wife are giving it." Mateo strolled back to the record player where a vintage Isaac Hayes cut played. "I can't risk Sanford being there with his wife on his arm while I come alone."

"I'm sure you won't be alone."

"Temple, please, you know I can't take any of them."

"Then take somebody new. With you there's always somebody new." She sighed while straightening magazines on the pine coffee table in front of the love seat.

"Temple, we both know Yates is no fool. Taking someone new won't matter. Taking you is the right move."

"Why?" Her hands stilled over the straightening.

Mateo went back to the kitchen for his juice. "You're my right hand. My go-to person. Taking you would keep it about business and not on some love affair, personal slant."

"Right." The disappointment flashed so briefly on her dark face that it could have been imagined. She chased the look away with a smug smile. "I must say that I'm impressed by your cunning thoughts," she teased.

"Well, don't sound so surprised." His tone was gruff.

"Hey, forgive me. I'm always surprised when you come up with complex plans without my help."

"Funny. So can I count on you to be there?"

Temple tapped her nails on her hip and considered the request. "Why not? But Taeo, even my attending a cocktail party won't mean much if there's nothing to follow it up with. We need to set meeting times to get all our ducks in a row for this survey expedition. We haven't even set up a date for that."

"Right." Mataeo grazed the back of his hand along the angle of his jaw. His mind had returned to the true business at hand. "Have you done anything with that yet?"

Temple smirked. "Since you gave it to me this morning? No."

"Watch it." He took his spot on the sofa and Temple followed suit. His thumb stroked the cleft in his chin as he watched her settle down next to him. The fabric of her housedress carried a light fragrance.

"First thing we need is a meeting of the crew. The crew chief especially." She tucked a few thick strands behind her ear. "Will you hire new people to handle this?"

Mataeo reclined on the sofa and brought his feet to the coffee table. "I don't see the need. We've got a top-notch crew—they can handle whatever I dish out."

"All right…" Temple reached for the notebook she kept on the high table behind the sofa and began to jot reminders. "Since we have no idea what the man needs to see, a brainstorming meeting with the crew is crucial." She chewed on the cap of the pen. "What's our time frame for this?"

"I think it plays in our favor to have Yates see things at the beginning stages and what lengths I'll go to ensure his clients are pleased."

"Hmm…" Temple's brows rose as she made the notation. "More great thinking— You really *are* impressing me."

"That's it." Mataeo grabbed a fistful of her housedress and made a play at attacking.

Temple moved quick and laughed all the way back to the kitchen.

"Yates needs to be there but I think it'd be good for Sanford to see the place, too."

Temple whirled around just after she cleared the doorway and brought both hands to her hips. "Are you insane?"

Mataeo placed his hands behind his head. "You know I am, but this isn't about that. I'm hoping to send a message."

"Which is?"

"Sanford's already intimidated by me—that's not overconfidence, that's fact," he said when she opened her mouth to argue. "When he sees what lengths North Shipping is willing to go to, he'll start making an even bigger fool of himself."

"Well then, the two of you will be a matched set because this is definitely your most foolish idea."

Temple continued to grumble in the kitchen while Mataeo hummed contentedly on the sofa.

Chapter 3

"These are standing meetings. Mr. North enjoys holding them over the course of each week with every department." Temple eased a sheet toward the young man seated next to her on the sofa in her office. "Your job will be to contact everyone and let them know what's on the agenda." She leaned back to judge his reaction. "I know this isn't quite as meaty as you were hoping for but it's a terrific way to familiarize yourself with such a large staff, which will definitely be important as you move up in this place."

"Ms. Grahame, this is fantastic." Edmund Jansen held the departmental list as if it were a priceless document. "I can't wait to get started."

Temple grinned and scooted closer to the coffee table for another portfolio. "Then let's move onto the layout of the meetings."

Temple and Edmund were wrapping up their conversation when Mataeo walked into the office.

Introductions weren't necessary; Edmund took care of greeting the boss and thanking Mataeo for giving him the chance to prove himself. Temple came to her feet slowly and watched Mataeo accept Edmund's adoration with a genuine smile. All the while she prayed the younger man's enthusiasm wouldn't have him blurting out the extent of his new chores for the boss.

"So what's up?" Mataeo closed the door behind Edmund when he left.

"Just wrapping up a meeting." Temple took folders from the coffee table and went about filing them in her desk.

"Kid seemed pretty excited about planning my events."

"He um…" Temple cleared her throat and wondered just how much Mataeo had overheard. "He'll just be handling a few things for me when I head down to Charleston. Remember I told you Mama's working with that Realtor?" She looked up at him from where she knelt near a desk drawer. "I want to be there."

"You sure there isn't any more to this, Temp?" He eased a hand into his pocket and moved closer to the desk. "If Miss Aileen needs my help—"

"She doesn't. I promise. Thank you, but it's nothing like that." She shut the drawer and stood. "Honest, Taeo, I'd tell you if it was."

"I don't get why *you* have to head down when there's plenty of family around."

"Because she's my mother," Temple snapped and then closed her eyes and produced a brief smile. "Nothing's gonna go lacking around here. I've got tons of people around to handle whatever you'll need." She appraised the walnut trousers and unbuttoned vest he wore over a cream shirt. "Sorry I haven't been able to find anyone to tie your ties but you'll survive."

Mataeo blocked her path when she moved from the desk. "I'm sorry." His sharp features had softened by concern. Lightly, he brushed his hand against her jaw. "I didn't mean to offend you."

"You didn't."

"Temple—"

"You didn't and I'm sorry I went off that way." She tapped her fingers along the side splits of the misty-blue skirt she wore.

"You deserved to go off." He took her chin between his thumb and forefinger while closing a bit more of the distance separating them. "You work your butt off around here. If anyone deserves to go home and see their mom, it's you."

"I'm still *very* sorry for snapping at you like that." Her entrancing eyes mirrored the concern in his.

It went without saying that Temple's apology was less about snapping and more about the fact that she had a mother to see. Mataeo had been alone since she'd known him. Shortly after their friendship began, it became clear that the subject of his family was off-limits. It was obvious, however, that he enjoyed the family element. He spent time with her huge tribe whenever he could. The Grahames and Hammonds of Charleston, South Carolina, loved him like he was one of their own.

Mateo kept his hold on her chin but caught her hand in his when she patted his chest. "Are you really okay?"

The gravel-toned voice tempered by softness stirred a reaction in places Temple decided it was best not to think of.

"I am." She nodded encouragingly. "I honestly am."

Mateo was not buying it, if the narrowing of his bedroom browns was any clue. He'd known her too long not to pick up on the weariness in her voice and bright eyes.

"Would you like me to put somebody else on this survey thing?"

Temple threw her head back and laughed. "I'm not about to put another poor soul in your line of fire. I promise it'll all be in place before my trip."

His smoky gaze grew dangerously narrow then. "I don't doubt you can handle it. I just don't want you overdoing it, all right?" He tilted his head but his eyes never left her face.

Temple, though, had lost her focus. No. No, she knew exactly where her focus was. It was on his hand smothering hers, his thumb soothingly albeit *innocently* brushing her palm.

"Temp?"

She prayed her lashes weren't doing their god-awful fluttering. "I'm good, please." She hoped her voice didn't sound like a moan.

"You're trembling." He released her hand to run his along the silver sleeve of her blouse. He frowned and tugged her closer.

That stirring reaction had become a dull throb in a place best not mentioned. Temple swallowed and tried to gently extract herself from his hold. "It's good you're here, though. We should talk a little more about these meetings."

"Hold it." His hand tightened on her arm and he drew her near until she was flush against his chest.

"Mataeo, I—"

"Shut up. I want you to come to me if you need to talk." His thumb began a maddening stroke of her elbow. "Don't ever think with all I've got going on that I don't have time for you."

Temple tried to laugh, but it came off as a nervous grunt at best. "I don't need to be handled, Taeo."

"But there are times when we could all use someone to listen." He squeezed both of her elbows then. "We're friends, aren't we?"

Temple knew she was forcing herself to nod. "Thank you." She went a step further and forced her mouth to curve into a smile. "I guess it's just getting everything arranged before the trip." She shrugged. "It's got me in a funk, but I'll be fine once it's all in place."

Accepting the excuse, Mataeo nodded slowly. "Well, I might be able to help you with that. We've got a meeting in ninety minutes with Ike Melvin, the crew chief."

"Oh, that's great!" Temple turned back toward her desk.

"Hey, hey." Mataeo caught her wrist. "Are we good here?" He smiled when she nodded, patted her hip and then he was gone.

Temple held her face in her hands.

Mataeo and Ike Melvin were already seated in the living area of Mataeo's office when Temple arrived for their meeting later that afternoon. Unhurried, Mataeo rose from his chair. He noticed how quickly Ike bolted to his feet to greet Temple. Mataeo strolled around to lean against the back of the sofa while Ike waved her farther into the office.

"Have you guys met?" Mataeo stroked the cleft in his chin as he inquired.

"Ike Melvin, Ms. Grahame."

"It's nice to meet you and please call me Temple." She accepted the hand he offered to shake. "I've heard good things about your work."

"Same here."

Mataeo rolled his eyes in response to the syrup dripping from Ike's voice. "We were just discussing the survey expedition," he explained when Temple glanced his way. "Shall we?" He headed back for his chair.

Temple took her place on the sofa, smiling when Ike joined her there. "So what have I missed?"

"Just prelims—who else from Ike's team you'd benefit from meeting with while trying to organize this thing." Mataeo angled his large frame to a comfortable position in the deep chair he occupied.

Temple nodded even as a frown came to her face. "Excuse my ignorance here." She shifted toward Ike. "As crew chief isn't meeting with you enough? You certainly know more about every aspect of the facility. I think you can give me all the information I need to prepare an effective survey agenda." She stopped short and studied both men. "Or am I wrong?"

Ike's hearty laughter livened the room. "I'm honored, Ms. Grahame—uh, Temple—that you consider me so knowledgeable." He waved toward Mataeo. "Have you ever told this lady how good she is for a person's ego?"

"I may've told her so on occasion," Mataeo coolly conceded.

"Well, I've done a little brainstorming." Temple opened the bound portfolio she'd brought along. "I realize this is basically a tour of the facility, but given that it's such an expansive site—maybe we should hone in on the most important areas."

"I agree." Ike leaned forward, bracing his elbows to his knees while resting a hand along the side of his attractive brown face. "This is actually where I feel my team could be most useful since they'll each be leading a specific area of the site. Maybe they could act as tour guides during the expedition—taking over the areas they'll eventually come to supervise."

"This is great." Temple nodded while jotting her notes. "Mataeo? You want to add anything here?"

"Sorry, man, didn't mean to run away with the conversation," Ike apologized, his gaze never leaving Temple's face.

"This makes organizing the tour so much easier," Temple continued to rave softly while writing in her pad. "It's a great touch and mixes things up, supplying information while giving Yates the chance to meet the people who'll hopefully be handling his clients. Mataeo? You can chime in anytime...."

Mataeo was more interested in the very obvious appraisal in Ike Melvin's gaze as the man watched Temple. Mataeo studied his crew chief with a combination of amusement and subtle surprise as if he couldn't quite believe how little Ike was doing to mask his attraction.

"Mataeo?"

He tuned into Temple's voice then, doing a double take when he looked at her. Something flickered in the deep warm pools of his stare.

Meanwhile, concern flooded Temple's expression. "Mataeo?" She leaned forward, frowning as he watched her like he'd never seen her before. "Are you okay over there?"

He smiled. "Yeah. Just thinkin'." He rested an index finger alongside his face. "Sounds like y'all got it covered."

Temple waited a beat, then fixed him with a curious smile before resuming her discussion with Ike.

Temple was still scribbling away at her pad some thirty-five minutes later. The meeting with Ike Melvin had provided her with a wealth of information to assist in creating an incredible agenda.

"We should meet again once I've put all this in place." She smiled at Ike. "You can let me know whether we need any changes or additions then. Does that sound good to you, Mataeo?" She frowned when he fixed her with a strange look. "Do you think Ike's crew should be here when we meet again?" Silence met her question. "Taeo?" She had her fingers poised to snap in front of his face.

At last he shook his head. "I honestly can't think of a thing to add here. It all sounds very good."

"Well." Temple scooted to the edge of the black leather sofa and stood. "Ike, it was nice meeting you."

She smiled when he stood to shake her hand. "I look forward to us getting together again."

Ike was already nodding. "So do I."

Mataeo massaged his neck, bowing his head to hide his smile. He figured Temple had no idea Ike wasn't referring to them getting together for business.

She walked by Taeo and squeezed his shoulder on her way past. "I'll see you later. Bye, Ike."

"Jesus." Ike lost some of his composure once he and Mataeo were alone in the office. He doubled over, bracing his hands on his thighs for a few moments. "How the hell do you keep it to just business with her bouncing around you all day?"

Mataeo headed for his desk. "She doesn't bounce." His rough voice sounded grim, monotone.

"You're right." Ike sighed, pushing both hands into his pockets while crossing the office. "She glides." He sat on the edge of the desk. "Hell, Taeo, she's amazing. I see why you never officially introduced me to her before now."

Practically speechless, Mataeo simply watched the man. He considered himself one rarely surprised by anything or anyone. But his crew chief had managed to accomplish that at least twice in one hour.

"It's okay." Ike waved his hands playfully. "I understand. I wouldn't want my friends knowing her, either."

"It's not like that." Mataeo sat behind his desk. "She sees who she wants, when she wants.…"

Ike braced his hands on the desk. "And how often is that when she spends most of her time working for you?"

Mateo couldn't prevent a smile from curving his mouth.

"Would you be upset if I asked her out?"

"Why should I be upset?" Mateo was unconscious of the clipped tone to his words.

Ike nodded, satisfied by the response at any rate. "Well, I gotta get goin'." He patted his khaki pockets for keys. "See you at the next meeting," he called on his way out the door.

Alone, Mateo dropped the cool facade. He sat on the desk, facing the view beyond the windows, and massaged a palm across his fist.

Later that afternoon, Temple was curled up on her office sofa reviewing notes from the meeting with Ike Melvin. Mateo found her when she was about halfway through.

"Don't get up." He raised a hand when she spotted him at the door and made a move to leave the sofa.

"I didn't mean to barge in." He motioned toward the door as he crossed the threshold. "Lilly wasn't at her desk," he said, referencing her assistant.

"Is everything all right?" Temple drew her knees up to her chest and watched him stroll in slowly.

"Yeah, fine." The quiet sandpaper tone of his voice held an absent quality. Hands hidden in the deep pockets of his walnut trousers, he perused the various knick-knacks and artwork lining the walls.

"Are *you* all right?" she rephrased, tilting her head just slightly when he picked up a photo of her with her sisters and studied it for the longest time. "Taeo?"

"Hmm? Yeah, yeah, Temp, I'm good." He set down

the photo and fixed her with a bemused look. "I think Ike's in love with you," he teased.

Temple chuckled, stretching her legs out across the sofa cushions and wriggling her toes. "He seems very knowledgeable *and* sweet. Glad I had the chance to meet him."

Mataeo felt his jaw clench over the "sweet" comment and wasn't sure he quite understood the reason why.

"Just remember you said that," he warned playfully, still trying to make light of the moment. "I got a feelin' the guy's leanin' toward asking you out."

"Hmph." Temple's focus had returned to her meeting notes. She looked up when Mataeo came to take a seat on the sofa.

Once settled, he pulled her feet across his lap before she could curl them beneath her bottom.

She gave him a nudge with one stockinged foot. "You're acting weirder than usual. What's up?" She nudged him again. "Taeo?"

A massive shoulder raised up beneath the crisp fabric of his shirt. His gaze remained downcast. "Just realized that I never ask you anything about that."

"About what?" Temple settled back against the arm of the sofa. "Ike?"

"About your personal life, Temp. About anything that doesn't have anything to do with *this* place." He grimaced and partly curved a fist. "Or about *my* personal life." In spite of his mood, Mataeo couldn't help but smile when he heard her laughter.

"And what a helluva personal life it is." She reached over to stroke the back of her hand across his cheek.

The smile curving his mouth didn't quite reach the

warm depths of his brown eyes. "I never meant to seem unsympathetic about it, you know?"

"About my…personal life?" She bit the corner of her upper lip when he nodded at her confirmation. "Well…" She smoothed both hands down the satiny length of her skirt. "I know it's practically nonexistent but I promise you it's not all *that* pathetic. There's no need for sympathy."

"I didn't mean it that way." His voice went softer. "I'm sure it's, um… I'm sure it's great. It'd have to be…" His fingers strummed across the top of her feet before traveling a bit higher.

Temple pressed her lips together and blinked several times in rapid succession. She tried to move her feet, but Mataeo prevented that.

"Are you sure you're okay?" She squeezed his wrists.

"I keep you so damn busy around here. *Way* too busy—not very fair of me." His eyes were narrowed as he sent her a sideways look.

"Taeo, no…I love it. I love my job." She ignored the little voice that reminded her that she was quitting.

"A girl can't spend her life working all the time, though."

"But I don't." She rubbed his wrist again, then drew back when she felt his hand constrict about her foot. "Do you think you're keeping me from having fun or something?" She moved her feet beneath her then. She scooted closer when she heard the gruff sound rumble in his chest.

"Taeo?" She dipped her head for a better look at his face. "Is this about my sex life or Manson Yates?"

"Jesus, Temple. Sex life?" His handsome features

contorted fiercely, as though that image was one he didn't want in his head.

His reaction gave Temple pause and she sat up a bit straighter. "Mataeo, why are you really here?" She ignored the voice that told her not to ask.

He captured her hand and dropped a hard kiss to the back of it. No words followed the gesture. Mataeo simply toyed with her fingers for a while. He repeated the hard kiss, only this time he planted it upon her mouth.

"I'll let you get back to work." He smoothed the side of his index finger across her parted lips. He kissed her again quickly and then left the office.

"Hey, did you already order?" Temple asked Megaleen as they hugged near the table Meg had secured in her uncle's seafood restaurant, Barnum's.

"You know I haven't." Meg rolled her eyes toward the front of the dining room. "Shane wanted to come take the orders personally when he found out I was having lunch with you. Told me I could just wait 'til you got here."

Temple laughed. Shane Barnum, the owner's son, had women all over Wilmington and beyond. Temple never took his advances seriously. The fact that Shane realized this made his attempts even more humorously outrageous.

"So what's going on?" Meg brought her elbows to the glossy oak table. "You sounded excited when you called about getting together for lunch."

"I talked to Kendall last night." Temple dropped her keys into her tote and set it on an empty chair at the table. "He found a place and claims I won't need to see another one once he shows it to me."

"That man." Meg flipped a lock of her auburn hair around her finger. "Always trying to outdo himself. I don't see how anything else could top the two places you already have."

"Well, Kendall told me he could handle those sales, as well." Temple reached for her water glass and took a hasty swallow.

"You're going to sell them?" Meg's brows drew close over her blue eyes. "Have you thought about what Mataeo will say?"

"No, I haven't, Meg. I never spend any time there. I feel like I've wasted his money...." She grimaced and pushed at the glass as if the water had left a sour taste. "I haven't spent a night in either place since he closed on them."

"I never knew that." Meg's fingers slowed in her hair. "Why not?" Her expression turned more probing when Temple only shrugged.

"There she is!"

Temple and Meg couldn't help but smile. Shane's charm was irresistible and he had them giggling like schoolgirls within a matter of seconds.

"Anything you want, lovely. Just ask."

"Cracked crab and lobster pulled fresh from the Atlantic no more than an hour ago," Meg requested in her most haughty tone.

Shane's stare matched the vivid blue of his cousin's eyes. "I said 'anything you want, lovely.'" He motioned toward Temple. "That would be her."

Generous laughter fell into place once more. It had

been weeks since Temple felt amusement at such a high level. That high lasted until she saw Mataeo walking past the columns guarding the entrance of the dining room. He wasn't alone.

"What is it?" Meg waited until Shane left with the orders. She'd noticed the shadow that had crossed her friend's face.

"Just hungry, that's all." Temple made pretense at studying the cuff of her blouse.

Meg turned in her chair to check the direction Temple had been looking. A thoughtful smile tugged at her mouth when she saw Mataeo North and his female lunch companion. Bowing her head, Meg traced the swirls in the oak table. Silence hung for a few minutes and then Meg leaned over to tap her fingers across the back of Temple's hand.

Meg squeezed until Temple met her gaze. Then she asked the question she already knew the answer to.

"You love him, don't you?"

Chapter 4

"'Course I love him." Temple didn't shrug off the question, but met it with sarcasm. "I've known him since—"

"Cut the crap, Temp. You know exactly what I mean." Meg leaned across the table again. "You're *in love* with him. Aren't you?" Her expression softened as she took note of Temple's reaction. "Honey, why does that upset you?"

"Are you crazy?" Temple's wilting expression turned stony. "How can you ask me that? You of all people know what it's like between the two of us. All the whispers, the rumor and innuendo that makes Mataeo look like the ladies' man of all ladies' men and me like a slut-come-lately."

"Sorry," Meg said as she laughed over the comparison.

Temple couldn't help but give in to a smile, as well.

Groaning, she raked her fingers across her thick tresses, drawn into a wavy chignon. "What good is it to love or be *in love* with him? What good is it to admit that I am or to even have the nerve to be happy about it? What good does it serve me?"

"That's why you're quitting, isn't it?" Meg's firm voice went soft and she trailed her nails along one of the swirls in the wood table. "None of this has anything to do with you being sick of the grind, does it?"

"God, Meg." Temple hid her face in her hands. "I love my job…a lot. I love all the demands, all of it…."

"Especially all those little *quirky* ones you have to fulfill for Mataeo." Meg kept her eyes on the table. "The ones that make folks think the two of you are sleeping together?"

Temple puffed out her cheeks while considering Meg's valid query. She supposed screening calls from jilted girlfriends, tying his ties, letting him have a key to her apartment, all the little handholds and familiar pats they exchanged were a bit rumor-inducing. She had honestly never given a second thought to them. She guessed Mataeo hadn't, either. Perhaps that was because it all came so naturally. Perhaps that was because there was far more than friendship at the heart of their involvement whether they realized it or not.

The water glass was sweating. Temple tapped her nails on the side until a bead of water slid across her finger. "This won't be as easy as I thought, will it?"

Meg's white wrap top crinkled near the shoulder when she shrugged. "I tried telling you that." She smiled up at the server who had arrived with their drinks.

"You don't know what this is like for me, Meg." Temple risked a quick glance at Mataeo across the room. "I swear I never meant for this to happen. I…" She frowned. "I thought I got past those feelings a long time ago."

"Oh, honey." Meg rubbed her hand across Temple's sleeve. "I guess it's hard to get over a man you're in love with when you see him every day."

"Yeah." Again Temple risked letting her eyes trail toward Mataeo and his lunch date. The woman looked vaguely familiar. *Hmph,* she thought. Probably one of the many bed warmers she'd had to give the boot on occasion.

"It'll be fine." Temple sighed and propped her chin on her hand. "Once this last deal is done, it'll be fine. I'll tell him my plans and that'll be that."

"Poor thing." Meg shook her head. "Still lyin' to yourself."

Temple pursed her lips. "I think I'll leave *you* with the check."

"Honey, that man is never gonna let you go. He depends on you too much and you know that." Meg paused to wave at a colleague she'd spotted across the room, but her attention quickly returned to Temple. "Whether his feelings are similar to yours, it doesn't matter. *Businesswise you're* his ace and I don't care how many people you put in place to handle all your responsibilities—it's gonna get messy if you try to leave him for good."

"That's silly." Temple waved off Meg's reasoning before propping her fist back against her cheek. "No one should ever think there isn't someone else out there who can do the job as well as them or better."

Meg spread her hands. "True. But when the *boss* thinks there's no one who can do your job as well or better than you, then all bets are off."

"Meg." Temple merely waved again, refusing to give merit to her friend's perception.

Across the room, Mataeo didn't appear at ease with the woman he dined with. The lunch meeting with H.R. Executive Liaison Cursha Wagner had been on his mind ever since he decided to call it over a week ago.

"So you're telling me she hasn't made any inquiries?"

"Mataeo." Cursha pressed her lips together and looked more than a tad uncertain. "I'm afraid I don't quite under—"

"Listen." He tapped an index finger on the table once. "What I'm saying to you is confidential. If I have any reason to suspect my concerns have been *discussed* in any way, shape or form—"

"Mataeo." Cursha's uncertainty faded and she sat up a little straighter in her chair. "There's no need to stress that. I'm good at my job and I certainly know better than to air the boss's laundry."

"Hell," Mataeo said and massaged the bridge of his nose. "Cursha, I'm sorry. Guess my concerns have me a little paranoid."

She nodded, her smile laced with understanding. "You're afraid you're about to lose your best person."

"She's my right arm." Mataeo's jaw flexed as the muscle there danced wickedly.

To himself, he acknowledged that she was a great

deal more than that. He couldn't function without her. He chose to shake off the thought in the back of his mind that challenged whether that "functioning" only pertained to business matters.

"I haven't had any conversations with her about her job or leaving it."

Cursha's words intruded on his thoughts. Mataeo nodded once quickly as though he were content.

"So…" Cursha tapped all ten fingers on the shellacked edge of the table. "Is this a onetime meeting or should I let you know if the situation changes?"

Mataeo focused on a spot near the edge of his tie. He didn't relish the thought of continuing down the path suggested by the liaison, but he hadn't gotten where he was by not following his instincts. Just then, his instincts were telling him that Temple was hiding something. He had no idea why he felt what she may've been hiding had anything to do with them. But when his instincts spoke, he had no choice but to listen.

Slowly, his mocha stare shifted toward Cursha. "Let me know," he said.

Temple returned from her lunch with Meg hardly able to recall how she'd gotten from her car to the office. The conversation with Megaleen still played hot and heavy in her brain. Whatever dramas might arise from her sudden departure, Temple knew that leaving was her only choice. If she ever expected to live her life without thoughts of Mataeo North as her lover instead of her colleague, she had to leave.

Meg was right. Being around him every day was not

easy. It was wrenching on her heart, her mind…other places she couldn't think of without moaning.

No one could deny how good she was at her job. It was difficult to be anything other than spectacular at it when she threw herself into it so deeply to avoid any other ideas from festering and stinging her heart. It helped…at work. Alone at home, those ideas took hold and stung until she refused to lie to herself any longer. Leaving was her best choice.

And what then? It was sure to be messy. There was even the chance of risking damage to their friendship. Temple slung her tote into an armchair and took refuge on the sofa. It was for the best. She buried her face in her hands and focused on the words. She needed a clean break…who the hell was she kidding?

An unexpected thud had her jerking up on the sofa. Her hands clenched at her sides as the office door opened and Mataeo strolled in wearing a frown. The tux he wore caught Temple's attention.

She didn't bother to move and simply waited for him to notice her on the chair. It didn't take him long.

"Let's make a move, Temp."

"A move to where?" She watched him warily.

"The cocktail party?" he said as though she should have remembered.

Temple pushed at her sleeve cuff to check her wristwatch.

"Yates asked for us to get there a little early—wants us to meet his wife." He shrugged indifferently.

The excuse on her tongue died. Temple stifled any refusal to the invite as it was business related. She stood quickly then, trailing her gaze over the devastating length of him in the gorgeous tux.

"I'll have to meet you there."

"We've gotta be early, Temp."

"Dammit." She closed her eyes and counted to three. "Mataeo, I haven't showered since this morning. And in case you haven't noticed—" she waved toward her clothing "—I'm not exactly dressed in formal attire. I haven't even thought about what to wear to this thing," she grumbled.

"That your bag?" He nodded toward the armchair he stood behind.

Temple only shrugged her confirmation.

He grabbed the tote like a sack of groceries. "You can help with my tie in the car. We'll take care of the dress first. Come on."

He was gone from the room before her mouth had the chance to fall open.

Temple barely had time to speak to Roland before Mataeo was hustling her into the back of the car. Speaking to the driver may have been out of the question, anyway, since Temple didn't know if she could even manage anything as simple as a greeting. She'd been pretty much speechless since Mataeo had ordered her from her office.

Still openmouthed, she eased across the cool seat and waited for him to settle in next to her. Waiting, it seemed, would be the order of things since no explanation was given with regard to their destination. Mataeo was on his phone before Roland even pulled the Maybach from the parking space.

Temple faced him more directly on the seat when she heard him speaking to the owner of her favorite boutique.

"That's right… Yeah, it's a cocktail party but they've asked the guys to wear a tux. Mmm-hmm… Yeah, I'm figuring formal but more on the casual side. Yeah… You've got her sizes and everything…" Mateo cast a cursory yet intense gaze along the length of Temple's legs. "Sounds good, we'll see you soon. Thanks, Laina."

Temple hit his arm the second he closed the phone. She felt a smidge of triumph when Mateo winced.

"What's the problem?" He rubbed the spot she'd pounded.

"Are we running so late that I don't have time to dress myself?"

"Dress *and* shower," he softly reminded her and propped a hand along the edge of his brow. "And you said you didn't even know what you were going to wear, right?" A massive shoulder rose lazily beneath his tailored jacket. "Just tryin' to speed things up a bit, Temp."

She rolled her eyes and reclined against the seat, feeling silly at continuing the argument. Instead, she watched him curiously for several seconds. "You're really taking this deal seriously."

Mateo flashed her a glare. "I take all my deals seriously."

"True, but I've never seen you jump through so many different hoops to sway a decision."

"And just how thoroughly did you read the file on Yates?" He regarded her with mild frustration clouding his striking honey-toned face. "Do you fully realize how much money and prestige acquiring this list could bring into the business?"

She raised his frustrated look with a mildly scathing one of her own. "The business has already got money and prestige. Sounds like this is about more than that for you."

Mateo clenched his jaw. "Manson Yates is revered in the shipping world, Temp." He appeared in awe of the fact. "A poor, unknown good ol' boy from the Tar Heel State who's now known the world over. Most of the time it takes having connects on the inside or a load of money or a combination of both to manage success like that."

He laughed and pressed his head against the padded rest on his side of the seat. "Why do you think rags-to-riches stories are so popular? It's not many of us who make it to that level, Temp."

She blinked, biting down on her lower lip and nodding as though finally comprehending what drove him. "You see yourself in him," she said.

Mateo shook his head against the rest. "I see what I hope to become." He drew a thumb across the sleek dark line of his brow. "Guess I think if Yates feels his carefully collected and managed list of clientele will fare well at North Shipping, then maybe I'm on my way to accomplishing that." He shrugged in a manner that confirmed he believed the reasoning would make little sense to anyone else.

Temple studied his sharply appealing profile just a second longer before turning her gaze outside the window.

* * *

The E. Fritz Dress Shop specialized in outfits for formal and semiformal events. The owner, Elaina Fritz, stood on her elegant, soft-lit sales floor and made easy conversation with her small, knowledgeable staff until she saw Mataeo and Temple walking into the shop.

"That's all right, Natalie. I'll see to these two," Elaina told the sales associate who was about to head over to the customers. She tugged the young woman's sleeve when she passed. "Commission's yours for being first on the greeting." She winked when Natalie beamed.

"Hey, you two."

Mataeo leaned close to kiss Elaina's cheek. "Nice move," he complimented her.

Elaina shrugged, but clearly appreciated his words. "Person's askin' for trouble if they don't treat their staff well." She pulled Temple into a quick hug before linking arms with her.

"So I've made some choices based on what Mataeo told me. I hope you'll see something you like. If not I've got lots more…."

Mataeo followed along behind the women. His focus had returned to his cell phone and he checked dates while deleting others. Elaina's sales staff was quite pleased by his preoccupation as it gave them the chance to observe him unaware. A few drew close to remark on his powerful build, beautifully emphasized in the professionally cut tux. Others were more interested in studying his incredible face.

Temple cast a glance across her shoulder. She was

also pleased to find Mataeo's attention directed on the phone. She brought her head closer to Elaina's.

"Could you please try to keep this little shopping trip just between us?" Temple whispered, giving an uneasy smile. "Mataeo's in a hurry and didn't want to wait around while I tried to make a choice out of my own closet."

Elaina chuckled and nudged her shoulder against Temple's. "Honey, it's fine. I'm definitely not gonna argue over helping myself make money."

"That's not it, E." Temple shook her head. "The boss buying a dress for his female employee could be misconstrued."

"Temple…" Elaina closed her eyes as understanding bloomed on her round cocoa face. She looked back at Mataeo before slanting Temple a wink. "Next to treating my staff superbly, *discretion* of the dealings of my clients is something I've definitely mastered. Right this way, Mataeo," she called just as he was finishing up with his phone.

Elaina showed them into a private dressing/showing room. There, she waved toward a rack filled with at least twelve dress selections.

"Have a look-see and just ring when you're ready." Elaina clasped her hands and smiled toward the row of dazzling choices. "Shall I send in an assistant for you, hon?"

"Oh, no, E. I'm fine." Temple was already sifting through the outfits with excitement and awe filling her lovely bright gaze. Her hands paused on one of the hangers and she turned toward Elaina. "These are incredible—thanks for putting all this together on the spur of the moment."

"Never a problem for my sweetest customer." The woman kissed Temple's cheek and then waved and turned for the door. "Just ring if you need me." She motioned toward the bell near the door.

Temple went back to studying the gowns but soon acknowledged Mataeo's presence. He'd made no move to follow Elaina from the room. As her hands stilled over the selections, she turned and offered a small smile.

"Thanks, Taeo, this was very thoughtful." She smoothed her hands down her sides while her brows rose expectantly. "I, um, I won't be long," she added, hoping he'd take the hint and leave her alone to change.

Instead, he closed the distance to the clothes rack. Temple watched as he browsed the items for a second or two.

"You're welcome," he said, turning to take her hands and squeeze. "Thanks for coming along."

She laughed then, humored by his words but also trying to make light of what was fast becoming an awkward moment for her. "Did I even have a choice?" she taunted.

"Yeah...I know I bullied you." He held both her hands in one of his and covered them with the other. "Sorry about that." The rough voice was scarcely a whisper.

"That's what I'm here for." She managed a faint smile.

"Right," he said, seconds before his head dipped and he kissed her.

She whimpered…. Yes, that was right—she whimpered the instant his mouth was on hers. Sure, they'd kissed before, but it was never more than a peck that lasted less than a second.

This kiss lacked any semblance of quickness and contained more than its fair share of intensity. His tongue engaged hers in a soft, almost hesitant dance, then withdrew seconds before she could become a more active participant.

Mateo cupped her chin and kissed the corner of her mouth, coolly avoiding the questions blazing in her brilliant eyes. He left the dressing room without a look back.

Chapter 5

Mataeo waited until he heard the shower running before he helped himself to a drink. The seal had not yet been broken on the new bottle of Jim Beam and he couldn't think of a better time to crack into it.

Tense conversations and situations were a given in his business, yet none of that compared to the tension swarming in the car as he and Temple made their way from E. Fritz to Temple's condo. He knew she had to be stunned and confused by what he'd done. He could say he felt much the same but that wouldn't have been completely true. Stunned? Not much. The kiss roused pleasures he wasn't surprised to discover were there.

Confused? No. He knew damn well why he'd kissed her. Those trusty *instincts* of his were bellowing that there was something up with her and that it would result in her leaving him. Another man? He couldn't be sure. Still, that possibility alone had forced him to finally acknowledge exactly what she meant to him—exactly what he wanted from her.

Now what? Confess his feelings? Tell her she was it for him? He muttered a curse and almost slammed his glass on the shelf housing the liquor. As a man who turned everything he touched to gold, a relationship was the *one* thing he couldn't make work. To try that with Temple only to fail could mean losing her as a friend.

Damn. He mouthed the word and set down his untouched glass. *Not* to try could mean the same and force him to watch her traipse off with some fool. He smirked then, smoothing a hand across soft close-cut waves of hair while admitting his arrogance.

He didn't even know if she felt that way for him. He had left without giving her an explanation for his actions or without waiting on her response to those actions. He'd caught her off guard, but she'd recover soon enough. When she did, there'd be questions, a slap to the face…or both.

There was nothing more to be done to the perfect coiffure she'd tamed her hair into. The dress was perfect, as well. It fit like a beautiful chiffon glove and the minor application of makeup was just right.

Still, she waited—er, *hid* in her bedroom. Nerves, confusion, arousal…they all swarmed like honeybees inside her stomach.

Where had that kiss come from? She knew Mataeo so well. At least she thought she did. There were times she knew his intentions better than her own, but she never saw this coming. Oh, yes…she'd hoped for it, but never had she let on to him that she did.

Her longings were kept tamped down and only acknowledged in the privacy of her home. She never even allowed them free reign inside her head at work. That was way too risky. Now she was holed up in her bedroom like an idiot because…why? She wanted him to tell her what his kiss meant or because she was afraid it meant nothing?

"Temp? We gotta hit the road!" he called out from the living room. She shook her head to ward off the deep thoughts. Standing at the vanity, she gave herself the once-over, grabbed her wrap and clutch and left.

Her breath caught when she saw him across the living room leaning against the bar. How was she supposed to act the part of the savvy executive when he'd just kissed her?

The jackass, he hadn't a clue or a care about what she went through because of him. Mataeo North, the man with scores of women at his beck and call, and he expected her to fall in line as one of them? Damn him.

Armed with the anger she felt she'd need to get through the evening, Temple braced herself and waited for him to meet her at the front door. When he stood next to her, she observed him for barely a second and then hauled off and slapped his face.

When she bolted out the door, Mataeo brushed the back of his hand across his jaw and smiled.

The phrase "the beautiful people have arrived" seemed a fitting summation when Mataeo and Temple stepped into Manson Yates's sunken living room. The area offered an otherworldly view of the Atlantic from a bay window that spanned an entire far wall.

Whether or not the couple realized it, there was an obvious flair between them. A spark illuminated and brought something sharp and lively to everything they said or did together. Just then, it was the mere act of walking into a room. In strappy glasslike heels, Temple stood practically eye to eye with Mataeo.

The flowing peach chiffon over the satin crème underdress of the gown accentuated Temple's rich coffee complexion and was yet another compliment to Mataeo's elegant tux and his gorgeous honey-kissed features.

"Wow," Temple breathed, looking up and all around as she turned to observe the lavishness. "I thought this would be a simple cocktail party."

Mataeo smirked. He observed the room, as well, but was more focused on the guests. "Man doesn't have the word *simple* in his vocabulary." He sighed and looked over at Temple. "Am I allowed to touch you?" He studied her with his deep stare, his gaze intent on her face momentarily before appraising the rest of her.

She wouldn't dare make eye contact and therefore she missed the study he made of her body. "Why should you stop now?" She swallowed when he pulled her hand through the crook of his arm.

Of course, if he *hadn't* been touching her there would have been cause for speculation as very well Temple knew. It was nothing for him to hold her hand or have one somewhere on her body. The gestures were blatantly protective and subtly possessive. She realized that and was well aware of the message it sent. Unfortunately, given the fact that she longed for his touch, urging him *not* to was something she'd been unsuccessful at doing. Speculation be damned.

It was easy for Mataeo to feel the tension beneath her skin where he held her. He knew they were going to have to discuss that kiss. By the time they got around to it, though, there would most likely be more than one that would need to be added to the conversation.

There was no time for that as Manson Yates was heading toward them. His arms were open and he wore a wide grin.

"Mataeo!" Manson brought a hard clap down on the younger man's shoulder. He then turned toward the stout, curvy woman at his side. "Kellie, this is Mataeo North. I told you about him. Mataeo, this is my wife, Kellie."

"I've heard a lot of great things about you, Mataeo."

"Same here, Mrs. Yates." Mataeo held one of the woman's plump hands inside both of his.

Kellie actually giggled while casting a sly look toward her husband. "I hope this man didn't bore you too much using me as a subject?"

Mataeo's lashes drifted down momentarily when he shook his head. "Not at all." His smile deepened. "I'd like you both to meet my CEO of North Shipping, Temple Grahame."

"Pleasure to meet you, Mrs. Yates, Mr. Yates." Temple smiled and shook hands with the couple.

"That's Kellie and Manson. That goes for both of you," Kellie softly instructed. Her blue eyes sparkled as she trailed a finger along Temple's chiffon sleeve.

"This is an absolutely lovely dress. Wherever did you get it?"

"I should apologize for how busy I've been keepin' y'all over there," Manson said once talk of fashion and boutiques had settled. "I've been mighty impressed."

Temple shook her head. "One should never apologize for giving us the chance to make more money.

"You have an incredible home here," Temple marveled once the laughter had circled among them for half a minute.

"How about a tour?" Kellie offered, her hands clutched in anticipation.

"Well, I—" Temple scanned the room. "Don't want to take you from your guests."

"They've got plenty to eat and drink. I'd say they're more than comfortable. Shall we?"

Temple accepted with a smile. She nodded toward the men and then followed Kellie. She was as eager to see the rest of the splendid house as she was to escape Mataeo's presence.

"North, she's stunning," Manson said after the women had disappeared into the crowd. "That face... she's got a body made for sons." He laughed, having caught the look of amusement on Mataeo's face.

"She's savvy, too," Manson added. "I see why you hired her. Savvy but it's understated—definitely there, though."

Mataeo had to laugh then. "No, you're right," he said when Manson looked surprised. "But she was barely here a minute. How could you tell all that?"

"Hell, son, that's when it's easiest to spot." Manson

pushed a hand into his trouser pocket. His handsome weathered face radiated a knowledgeable look. "It's understated *and* a part of who she is. There's no need for her to go overboard proving she's smart—her intelligence follows her like mist. Hmph." He folded his arms over his chest. "I've been able to spot more idiots during a two-minute conversation than a weeklong conference. Doesn't take long for an idiot to call attention to hisself."

"So I'm beginning to realize." Mataeo smirked, having spotted Sanford Norman across the room.

"Is there more with you and her than business?"

Mataeo laughed again. "No, sir, it's strictly business." *Or it was,* he tacked on silently.

"That won't last long."

Mataeo coughed over the prediction. "Mr. Yates—"

"Ah, ah, ah—Kellie said to call us by our firsts."

Grinning, Mataeo shook his head and considered his next words. "We've been friends a long time…now colleagues."

"And that's exactly my point." Manson paused to accept a fresh drink from a passing server. "It's gettin' to you now. It's written all over you—all over you both." He patted Mataeo's arm and then walked on.

The next forty-five minutes were blissfully business-like. Yates called an impromptu meeting, which many of the guests were happy to attend.

Though she was the only woman at the meeting, Temple was at ease. Without batting an enviably lengthy lash, she proved that she was well versed on what North Shipping could offer Yates World and why Yates World was perfect for their company.

Mataeo occupied the cream leather armchair that matched the one Temple had claimed. While she spoke, he took the time to observe the group, who practically clung to her every word. He set his stare on the wheat-colored carpeting and wondered how much of the group's "interest" had to do with the facts and figures she spouted. She'd been his confidant for years and he'd taken pride in the fact that he hadn't allowed anything to overshadow that.

And what about now? He studied the glasslike slipper encasing her foot as it swung back and forth. Coolly, he aligned his index finger along the corner of his eye and subtly observed the airy flutter of her gown. The movement stirred the light scent of her perfume.

God, he was in trouble.

Sanford Norman appeared to be the only man immune to the charm of Mataeo's beautiful associate. He spent his time challenging Temple's thoughts on North's supposed superiority to S. Norman Freight.

"I'm sure we're all quite impressed by your *talk,* Ms. Grahame, but in our business action and know-how is what counts most."

"I agree." She offered a curt nod and no hesitation. "I also believe it's important to put our *action* in gear right behind the chitchat." She smiled at the taken-aback look that covered Sanford's face. She dismissed him and smiled toward the other meeting participants. "I look forward to seeing Mr. Norman and the rest of you at the survey expedition we're putting in place to showcase new facilities acquired with Yates's clientele in mind. Members of our on-site crew will be there to showcase their 'know-how.'" She smiled at Sanford and then stood.

"If you all will excuse me—" Temple reached for her glass and twirled the ice around "—I'd like to freshen my cocktail."

Every man in the room stood as Temple made her exit.

"Damn," someone muttered when the study door closed behind her.

A while later, the party was showing signs of winding down. Temple had ventured out to the balcony, determined to lose herself in the view of the night skies sparkling over the Atlantic.

As the party was nearing its end, Temple thought of taking a cab home. Surely that would only increase the tension quietly residing between her and Mataeo. Murmuring an obscenity then, she banged her fist against the wrought-iron balcony edge. This was the thing she'd feared, the thing she didn't want to happen. The thing she'd done her best to avoid was suddenly staring her right in the face.

She'd fought so diligently to keep their friendship just that. Now, it was dangerously close to becoming what she'd found herself craving more and more over the years that she'd known him. How long had she harbored those feelings? she wondered. Since the night he'd saved her from suffering a horrible fate at the hands of a date who didn't understand the word *no?* Perhaps. Perhaps since that very night she'd been falling irresistibly in love with him.

She smiled at her own ignorance and fixed her sights on a star winking far away. The fact that this situation would turn ugly was a given. She should have prepared herself better. But had it really turned ugly? He'd kissed her, after all. *But* he didn't know that she was plotting to leave him. Yes, ugliness was definitely still on the horizon.

Temple was easing back from the ledge with intentions of turning and heading back into the waning party. Before she could turn, a hand appeared on either side of her along the ledge.

"Are you about to tell me what the hell it is you think you're doing?" she asked, hoping she'd forced enough steel into her voice.

Mataeo took his time answering. He smoothed the back of his hand across her shoulder blades and followed the move with a guarded, intense look. "Would you believe me if I told you I didn't know?" he asked her finally.

She turned in the circle of his loose embrace. "No. No, Mataeo, I wouldn't believe that. You don't do anything without a reason." She cocked her head at a saucy angle and made a curious study of his face. "Was this all just to put me in character for tonight? Make a good show for Manson Yates?"

"What the hell?" His expression was suddenly murderous. One hand left the ledge to grip her arm tightly over the delicate chiffon. "Is that what you think?" The raspy quality of his voice harbored something more sinful when he whispered the words, "Is that how you believe I see you? As something I use when I feel like it?" He gave her a small tug. "Is that what you've thought of our relationship all these years?"

"No." Temple closed her eyes as if suddenly weary. "It's not what I think or—or what I've *ever* thought. But, Mataeo, you can't expect to…kiss me out of the blue and not have me confused by it." She pressed her lips together and stood transfixed by the next change in his expression.

The anger seemed to curb. Something else she couldn't identify eased into place and she stiffened beneath his hand on her arm.

"Didn't you enjoy it?"

She blinked. "What?" The word came out harsh.

A rakish element belied the warmth of his cocoa gaze. "It's a simple question, Temp. Did you enjoy it?"

"Mataeo, what is going on with you?"

It didn't take much for him to invade her space. He only stepped a tad closer. "Answer my question."

She closed her eyes while waving both hands about her head. "I can't talk to you when you're talking crazy."

"Answer it," he demanded, shifting his weight, which easily thwarted her attempt to move past him.

"Mataeo, don't do this."

"Why?" He smiled when she looked at him. "Because you *did* enjoy it?"

"Taeo…"

"Answer me, Temple."

"I can't. Let me by."

"In a minute."

He was kissing her again, full-blown and far more erotically than he had earlier that day. He wasted no time with tenderness then and simply took—drinking in the sweetness from her mouth, silently daring her to deny she was most definitely enjoying it. His arm, resting on the balcony ledge, circled around her waist— a bit of added insurance that she wouldn't move from where he wanted her.

Thoughts of moving away—of resisting his kiss— were far from Temple's mind. She participated enthusiastically, hungry for his tongue manipulating hers into an increasingly fiery play. Happily, she lost herself in the pleasure he roused.

Mataeo brought an end to the scene despite the fact that his position was suddenly less than advantageous. Temple had him practically flush against a brick wall and her fingers were tugging at his bow tie.

"Temp…" His hand flexed on her hip, keeping her close even as he ordered his hormones to cool. "Honey, let me take you home."

Temple acknowledged her inner voice of common sense then. "We can't, Mataeo…."

He chuckled over her misunderstanding. "I won't try anything. I promise." His rough voice carried a soothing lilt. Gently, he set her back, used his thumb to brush at the faint smudge of her lipstick. He then bumped her chin with his fist, waited patiently for her eyes to meet his and then he escorted her from the balcony.

They didn't notice Sanford Norman as he watched them from a shadowed corner.

Chapter 6

Temple woke and took a deep breath. She closed her eyes when she realized it *was* the next morning and that the previous night was joyfully over and done with.

Relieved, she told herself that the weirdness of the previous day was the only reason everyone was acting so—well…weird. *Yes, yes that fit,* she thought. Such an unorthodox day was the only thing that had Mataeo kissing her like they were—

The thought made her moan and she closed her eyes again briefly before whipping back the covers. She bolted from her room and headed straight to the kitchen for a glass of juice.

Faint streams of dawn illuminated the condo, leaving off the need for lights. She was glad. Lights would have only ushered in the day too quickly—too boldly. She wasn't fully ready to face it yet.

Temple downed half a glass of orange juice right

there at the fridge. She guzzled the rest while making her way down the hallway and back into her room. She set the tall glass on the nightstand before flopping down into the tangled covers.

The sound of running water caught her ears and she bolted up in the center of the bed. Eyes trained on the bathroom door, she waited and watched Mataeo stroll out as though it was the most normal thing in the world.

"Morning," he greeted her with an easy grin.

"What are you doing here?" Thick tufts of hair flew into her face when she shook her head. "I thought you left…." Quickly, she recalled the events of the night before. He'd brought her back to her place. She'd headed right for her room and…assumed. She'd assumed he'd shown himself out.

Leaning against the dark maple dresser, Mataeo patiently waited. His smile deepened as he watched her work the matter out in her head.

"I just decided to stay over," he explained when she looked up at him openmouthed.

Temple blinked, bowing her head to ward off the incredibly alluring sight of his broad and perfectly cut chest. "You can't do that, Taeo," she groaned.

Mataeo began a slow stroll to the bed, but stopped when she moved closer to the headboard. "Why not?" he challenged. "Why can't I? I do it all the time."

She wouldn't look his way. "You can't anymore."

"Why not?"

"Mataeo…you kissed me."

"And you kissed me back—twice."

Finally, she met his gaze. "Then you understand why you staying over is… We can't."

He was on the bed then. His big frame crowded her, leaving no space for retreat. "We can do anything we damn well please."

"*You* can." She rested back on the headboard and shrugged. "*I* can't."

Mataeo averted his gaze, regarding her words in silence while smoothing a hand across his soft hair. Finally, he raised one shoulder in a lazy shrug. "Well then."

He was kissing her—again and *again* she kissed him back. It was foolish to even think of resisting. What for? This was all she dreamed of. Still, she made a weak effort at doing so when he released her mouth to trail his down her neck and across her chest.

Sadly, the "wait" she'd intended to utter had no volume and simply left her lips in the form of yet another moan. Overwhelmed and aroused beyond belief, Temple tugged him closer. She snuggled into his magnificently sculpted body when he settled between her thighs.

She instigated the next kiss with no intentions of stopping. Hungrily, she thrust her tongue deep, whimpering with every lunge she made into his mouth.

Any decisions of stopping would have to be made by Mataeo. The ability to exercise a cooler head would not be easy considering he'd been offered a taste of a treat he never knew existed. The fact that the treat went by the name of Temple Grahame put it all on an even more incredible level.

Exercising superhuman willpower, he managed to keep his touch to the top of her pajamas and panties. He *just barely* managed....

Temple threatened to break the skin on her lip when she bit hard to stifle her demands that he do more. Grazing her nails down his back, she linked her legs about his waist and lost herself in what she'd only dreamed of for years.

The foreplay had become too heated, even by Mataeo's standards. He couldn't think straight he wanted so badly to be inside her. *That* was dangerous. Far more dangerous than what they'd already done. He buried his face in the side of her neck, inhaling the natural provocative scent of her. The thrusts he drove against her were mere mimics of what he needed. And she was doing nothing to sway him from going after his needs.

"Temp…" His teeth latched onto her earlobe. His hands curved beneath her pajamas to cradle her ample bottom. "Temple, I need to…stop…."

"Mmm-hmm…" She arched into him before writhing her hips against his. Her nails grazed the broad plane of his chest, stopping briefly to flick her thumbs across his nipples.

"Temple." Mataeo closed his eyes tightly, digging deep for just a shred of resistance. Finding it, he folded his hands over her wrists and tugged. When her exquisite hazel gaze was focused on him, he dug for more resistance.

"I'll see you later, all right?" He nodded as if to rouse her encouragement.

"Sure you will." Temple's expression was soft as she studied him. "We've got more work to do, don't we?"

Mataeo rolled his eyes as a groan worked its way up through his chest. Wearily, he rested his forehead on her shoulder.

"Hell," he growled when he felt the subtle moves of her rubbing against him. Before his body temperature could rise another notch, he pulled away and left the room.

Temple turned onto her stomach and waited. Five minutes passed before she heard her front door slam.

As usual, Temple was first to arrive for the monthly departmental meeting. The gathering with the operations staff was set to begin in less than ten minutes. Temple was seated in her usual spot near the head of the table when Mataeo arrived.

"Well…" Surprise illuminated her coffee-brown face. "This is a shock. You're never early," she teased, hoping to keep some semblance of their usual manner. She released a small sigh, noticing that a tie hung loose around the collar of the charcoal-gray shirt he wore.

"Hey?" Mataeo settled his hands on her hips when she moved closer to fix his tie. "Are you okay?"

"I'm fine." She tried to laugh.

His grip firmed and he took a seat on the conference table.

Temple could practically feel his gaze on her. The intensity of it told her that he didn't believe her.

"I'm just fine, Taeo," she sang. "It's not like you forced me or anything." She cleared her throat when his hand flexed at her hip.

Mataeo's jaw muscle twitched and his gaze faltered just a bit. "You know I'd never do that."

"And you didn't." It was becoming increasingly difficult to maintain a chipper tone. Frowning then, she gave the tie an unnecessary jerk.

Mateo pulled her hands away.

Temple knew him well enough to read the silent request. "I'm fine and you didn't force me. Now, can I please?" She flexed her hands above where he held on to her wrists. He released her and she finished the tie. The task proved to be more difficult than all the times she'd ever done it before.

The intensity of Mateo's stare never waned. He studied her closely while she worked. Hands still at her hips, his eyes drifted across her face before lowering. The warm chocolate depths lingered at the opening of her maroon pin-striped blouse before he started a slow kneading of her waist and hips.

Temple wanted to close her eyes and savor mounting sensations. Bad idea. Especially when the room they occupied was moments away from being filled to capacity.

She secured the knot and smoothed her hands briskly across his shoulders. Mateo tightened his hold before she could move.

"This isn't the time, Taeo."

"Because we're about to start a meeting." He leaned in to voice the question close to her ear.

Temple smirked. "Because of a lot more than that." She brushed her thumb across the seductive curve of his mouth and moved back just seconds before the first meeting attendees arrived.

Chapter 7

"If we weren't friends, I could retire off all the billable hours our meetings are incurring." Megaleen commented when she saw Temple taking the bar stool next to her.

"I want to up my timetable." Temple slung her tote on the cherrywood bar top and then rested her forehead on the backs of her hands.

Meg peered around to get a look at Temple's face, but she was unsuccessful. "Timetable?"

"For leaving, Meg. I want to move it up."

Rolling her eyes then, Meg snapped her fingers for the bartender, who had been chatting with customers at the other end of the counter.

"Tequila. Two double shots."

"Meg—"

"Hush." Meg nudged Temple's shoulder with her

own. "It might relax you enough to tell me what the hell happened."

"It's gonna take more than a double shot, then." Temple released a makeshift laugh. "I have no idea what happened."

"Okay…" Meg chewed her lip thoughtfully. "Is there any sort of beginning you could possibly start from?"

"He kissed me."

Meg needed no further clarification. She leaned against the back of the bar seat. The bartender sat down the drinks and she downed the first before he provided the second. "How?" she asked finally.

Temple lifted her head and had to smile. "I'd think *you* of all people would understand the mechanics of that."

Meg replied with a withering look.

Temple sighed, quickly losing her taste for humor. Nursing her first shot of tequila, she told Megaleen about the cocktail party and the dress.

"Twice?" Meg took a smaller sip of her second shot when Temple told her about the kiss on the balcony.

"Yeah, the um…the second time I was a lot more eager." She groaned and finished off her first drink. "Then there was the um…third time in my bed the next morning." The liquid stung the back of her throat and she smiled when Meg appeared to be choking on her drink. "I can't believe I did that—you'd think I'd never been kissed before. I mean, at the party I had him pressed against the wall for God's sake! In my room…I didn't want him to go."

"And?" Amused, Meg shook her head. "Sweetie, the man is a dream. A woman would have to be made out of steel not to feel some kind of tingle if he looked her way."

"Right." Temple traced her nail around the rim of the empty glass. "It's because I've avoided those *tingles* that I've been able to keep myself out of the stew for as long as I have." She focused on the oversize pearl button on the cuff of Meg's blouse. "I haven't been able to look at him in two days."

"But isn't this what you've wanted? You *are* in love with him, right?"

Temple laughed and finished her second shot without batting an eye. "I love him…and as for his actions lately being what I want, that gets a yes and no answer." Laughter across the bar area captured her interest for a few moments. "It's like drooling over some guy in a movie or a magazine." She grinned at Meg. "You think about what you'd do if you ever met him, but you don't really ever expect to meet him, dammit."

Meg smoothed back a coarse lock of Temple's hair left dangling from the side-swept chignon she wore. "So you're content loving him from afar and suffering for him alone?" She fluttered her lashes theatrically when Temple flashed her a look.

"It's not about being content. It's about being afraid."

"Of Mataeo?"

"Of his ways." Temple pushed at her empty shot glasses. "You forget, Meg, that I've had a front-row seat to all of his relationships over the years. I know what's in store for a woman once he's…had enough of her."

"Temple…" Meg had the look of a person who'd just solved a riddle they should've guessed the answer to long before. "You being upset…it's got nothing to do with what people will think about you and Mataeo as a couple, does it? You're worried about how you'll handle it if he ever gets tired of you."

Clearing her throat, Temple waved off the bartender when he made a move to refill her glass. "What people think is definitely a part of it. I really don't need *that* headache." She tugged the hem of the burgundy vest she wore. "The speculation that always follows us will definitely go into overdrive then." She shivered as if chilled by the thought.

Meg laid a hand over her wrist. "But that's not the biggest part of it? Honey, aren't you expecting too much of the worst?"

"That's funny." Temple's voice was dry but she did laugh. "Mataeo can't hide what he is. Not even from me. It's not in his nature to commit to one woman."

"Not even when that woman is his best friend, confidant, top business associate and only family he's got?"

"And I can't risk losing any of that." Temple's light gaze harbored a poignant tinge.

Mataeo raised his hand but didn't make eye contact with the server in the brightly lit executive café of North Shipping. He and Temple met there with Ike Melvin and his team. Most of the attendees for the business luncheon couldn't stop raving over Temple getting the survey expedition agenda together so quickly.

"Well, you guys should really give most of the credit to your boss." Temple folded her arms across her beige wrap blouse and smiled in Ike's direction. "All of his input at our first meeting set me in the right direction for putting all this in place."

"Temple, please don't," Geoffrey Cage drawled in dramatic fashion. "If you get him thinkin' he was responsible for everything comin' together, he'll make workin' for him sheer hell!"

Laughter roared outrageously at the table, but it was all in fun and relief. Everyone knew how important the deal was for the company and they had worked diligently to ensure all aspects were just right.

Mataeo constantly observed his employees. His focus, however, was more centered on Temple and Ike. Mataeo brushed his thumb across his mouth as it curved into a faint, knowing smile.

Temple was more animated than usual, he noted. Of course, Ike and his team could set anyone at ease, but the fact that she hadn't looked his way in over a week left him uneasy.

His fist clenched and he moved it from the table to rest along the crease in his navy trousers. Tension between them—*further* tension was the last thing either of them needed. Kissing her had been a mistake and it was setting in motion events that could be their downfall in so many ways.

He thought back to the first day he'd kissed her. Mataeo knew, regardless of the consequences, it was a mistake he'd make all over again.

"Well, everything looks good to us." Ike nodded toward his team surrounding the table. "We're all set on our end to greet the group and offer a thorough tour of the site. So long as the boss is good with it, we can get the ball rolling."

Everyone looked to Mataeo, who had come out of his pensive shell and rejoined the discussion.

"Will it be a problem to set it for the beginning of next week?" he asked, watching the group exchange eager glances.

Ike spread his hands and shrugged. "Sounds good to us."

"What have we got open, Winnie?" Mataeo turned to the petite secretary who'd diligently scribbled away notes since the meeting began.

Winnie Osmond nodded as Mataeo tossed out dates. She smiled, on the verge of gushing when he leaned close and said something only she could hear.

Temple looked up in time to catch the exchange. She stilled, watching the couple more closely than before. She caught herself, but not before Mataeo caught *her* staring. Luckily, Ike was calling to her before anything more could come of it.

"I know we probably won't see much of each other once this tour's over." Ike spoke below the hum of the various conversations at the table. "You'll be back in your cushy office and I'll be back in the trenches."

"Don't even try it." She rolled her eyes while brushing her fingers against the back of his hand. "I've seen *your* cushy office and you don't spend all your time in the trenches, either."

"All right, all right you got me." He grinned and then lowered his gaze and grew serious. "But our offices are pretty far apart, so the chances aren't good that we'll see each other as much as we have over the last few weeks."

She nodded. "I see your point."

Ike leaned closer. "Would I be out of line if I asked to see you—out? Socially."

Temple couldn't resist smiling at his nervous manner. She shrugged. "I think I'd like that."

"Would anyone like dessert?" The waiter had returned to the table.

Mataeo clapped his hands. "Everybody eat up. I'm payin'."

Orders ran high for the taste of one of the delectables from the dessert menu. While the group was busy making selections, Mataeo left his place at the table and walked around to Temple's.

"Would you come with me?" he asked once she'd acknowledged his squeeze on her shoulder.

Temple stood and dutifully followed. She didn't think to question their destination until she noticed they were venturing quite a ways off. Mataeo didn't stop until they were in one of the elaborate unisex bathrooms off the dining area.

"I'm taking a chance that talking's allowed again." He twisted the bolt on the washroom door. "Back there at the table was the first time you've looked at me in days."

"Mataeo, what—"

"Stop." He raised a hand but didn't look her way. "You know good and damn well what I'm talkin' about."

"And you're one to talk—complaining about *my* behavior? Please." She rolled her eyes and planted her butt on the edge of the marble countertop.

"I'm not complaining, Temp." Mataeo took a moment to work the tension from the bridge of his nose.

"I know I'm to blame for things goin' weird between us but I can't go back and change it." He waited a beat. "I wouldn't change it if I could."

"Why are you doing this?" She bowed her head, holding it between her hands. "Why now?" she moaned.

Mataeo shrugged and leaned back against the door. "Guess it's all that crazy talk about relationships that finally got to me."

"So? Why come after *me?*"

"Temple." His mocha stare sharpened in disbelief. Muttering a low curse, he ran a hand across his head. "Who else would I *come after?*"

"Are you kidding me?" She straightened on the counter. "Need I remind you of your long and varied array of volunteers? I'll bet the line could start right out there at the lunch table and stretch on for miles— at least on *this* coast, anyway."

Mataeo's sharp stare suddenly took on a new aspect. One that was subtly playful and unmistakably danger- ous. "Are you talking about Winnie? Temple? Are you jealous?"

"Are *you?*" She left the counter. "Is this little bath- room break about Ike asking me out?"

"Did he now?" Mataeo whispered, smiling when Temple closed her eyes as though she realized she'd said more than intended.

"Mataeo, stop this, please?" she urged, her voice soft as she moved closer. "We can't afford to play this game—especially not now."

The playfulness left his eyes, yet the danger re- mained. "What's so special about the timing?" He tilted his head to maintain eye contact every time she would try to look away.

"Have you forgotten about this deal we're trying to close? We need all our focus and everyone else's on that."

"Right."

She was rolling her eyes in reply to his sarcasm just as her phone rang. Grimacing, Temple pulled the device from her skirt pocket, intending to shut it off. She paused when she saw Kendall Ingram's name. She returned the phone to her pocket and Mataeo caught her arm. Keeping the vice grip on her arm, he guided her back to the counter.

"I have the strongest feeling that you're keeping things from me and that it's about more than Yates and his relationship crap."

Temple swallowed. She'd known Mataeo long enough to recognize temper stirring in his eyes.

"You of all people know all too well how much I dislike being kept out of the loop."

"Dammit, Mataeo, *what* do you think I'm keeping from you?"

His smile held no humor. "I don't know yet. For your sake, I pray you tell me before I find out on my own."

Temple wrenched her arm out of his hand and stormed from the washroom.

"Idiot," Mataeo whispered, berating himself for a foolish loss of control, and losing it with Temple of all people. He braced his fists against the counter for a few seconds, and then smirked as he pulled his phone from his jacket pocket.

"Might as well go all the way," he declared while

searching and then selecting the number he wanted from the cell phone. He wasted no time with greeting the person who answered. "Find out who Kendall Ingram is."

Chapter 8

Winnie Osmond was quickly working her way up through the ranks of North Shipping. She wouldn't be part of the secretarial pool for long.

Temple knew this, of course. She'd had her eye on the young woman far longer than the lunch meeting the day before. Temple had been watching Mataeo and Winnie so closely because she'd toyed with the idea of approaching the girl about taking over some of her *responsibilities* for the boss. Perhaps finding Mataeo someone new to tie his ties wasn't so far-fetched, after all.

The both of them had been in Temple's office confirming attendees to the survey expedition. Winnie's efficiency had made the task far easier on Temple than she'd hoped for. Winnie's work had been so efficient, in fact, that all Temple needed to do was go through the information cards and make note of the various aspects of the expedition. Temple took note of what the attendees were most interested in learning more about.

"Winnie, this is fantastic." Temple never looked away from the card she held. "You've really made this easy for me. I hate doing everything electronically."

"Thanks, Ms. Grahame. Thank you so much." Winnie's huge brown eyes sparkled vibrantly from her round face. "I know how much you've got on your plate. And you make it look so effortless. I still don't know how you make it all work."

"I'm glad I have everybody fooled," Temple drawled. Once their hearty laughter had settled, she added, "I promise you it ain't easy."

Winnie tugged a curly brown lock of bobbed hair behind her ear. "I know and if I had any doubts about that, I definitely don't after this project for the survey."

"Mmm…was it anything like what you expected when I first approached you about handling it?" Temple kept her eyes focused on the attendance cards.

Winnie's eyes merely brightened. "Oh, Ms. Grahame, it's been incredible! I mean, I'm still so thrilled by the fact that you all even wanted me on it." She looked up in awe, studying the track lights that provided soft illumination from the ceiling. "I got so deep into this, I didn't even realize how much time had passed once I was done."

Temple glanced up in time to see the sudden look of unease flash over the face of the young Caucasian woman. "What's wrong?" she asked.

"It's just…" Winnie pressed her lips together. "I hope my excitement over the project didn't cause me to rush it. I'm pretty sure I handled everything, but still…you guys are the experts."

"Well, Winnie." Temple gave a theatrical sigh and waved her hand over the cards. "So far I can't see where you've left any detail overlooked." She leaned back on the sofa and let one strapless heel swing back and forth. "I see all the information I requested and you've even added remarks from the attendees. That'll give the tour a more personal touch that'll carry everything over."

Winnie's apprehension faded, allowing joy to once again take its place.

Temple left off her study of the cards and regarded the young secretary more closely. "How would you feel about taking the lead on more projects like the one you just finished?"

Winnie's mouth was the size of a small O. "Well, I—yes! Yes, Ms. Grahame, of course."

"Now listen, I want you to understand that while you may not have to work so often on your own, there will be more input and expectations from Mr. North."

"Right." Winnie's nod was pert as she fiddled with the pleats in her knee-length black skirt. "So I'll, uh— have the chance to work more with him, then?"

"That's right." Temple rearranged the attendance cards unnecessarily. "Would that be okay with you?" She knew she didn't need to ask. The girl's fluttering lashes and the smile she was biting her lip to hide were answer enough.

"We'll talk about it more later." Temple decided she'd showered the young woman with enough excitement for one day. "I'm gonna finish up here and I'll buzz you if I have any questions, okay?"

"Yes, Ms. Grahame." Winnie beamed as she stood. "Thank you, Ms. Grahame," she said and all but floated from the office.

Alone, Temple shook her head and smiled. Her guess was that Winnie Osmond would have one hell of an evening bragging to her friends about the mere possibility of working side by side with the great and sexy Mataeo North.

Temple couldn't blame her. She'd been just as giddy upon landing her first *real* job out of college, too.

Of course, Winnie's excitement had more to do with her working alongside Mataeo himself than with a career coup. Even still, Temple couldn't blame the girl. Hell, if she herself hadn't been so jaded by that age, she may have turned somersaults when a gorgeous man threw more than a nod in her direction. Thankfully, those days were long gone and best forgotten.

She sighed, easing back to reality and finding Mataeo on the edge of the coffee table directly in front of where she sat on the sofa.

"Dammit, Mataeo…" She cursed herself for jumping and wondered if she should tell him how nerve-racking it was for a big man to move around so undetected. Her guess was he already knew.

"Something wrong?" She straightened on the sofa, smoothing nonexistent wrinkles from her dark flare-legged trousers.

"Passed Winnie in the hall." He smirked, throwing his gaze toward the door as if he were envisioning the encounter. "She seemed excited. More excited than usual, that is. Said she completed the project and how happy you are with her work. I think you've got a fan."

"Hmph." Temple stood from the sofa, missing Mataeo's gaze raking the length of her body. "It's not *me* who she's a fan of." Soft laughter carried over her shoulder.

"She also said she's looking forward to working with me more." Mataeo left the coffee table and slowly crossed the distance to the desk.

"That's nice." Temple's easy expression sharpened just a smidge. She made a pitiful show of looking for something on her desk.

"Mmm-hmm." Mataeo took his preferred spot on a corner of the desk. "According to Winnie, *you* asked her about it and she can't wait."

"That's right." The ability for Temple to hold on to her indifference was fading. "I think she'd be just right for handling some of my tasks while I'm down in Charleston. Remember I told you I'd be gone awhile?" She straightened, expectancy shining in her hazel eyes. "You're gonna need someone to handle whatever comes up."

Mataeo kept his cool position on the desk. He studied his palms, rubbing one across the other and appearing anything but relaxed.

"You talk like you're going away forever." He didn't care if she heard the grit in his voice. Mataeo shifted on the desk and repeated the words when Temple didn't provide a quick enough response. The grit in his voice was undeniable then.

"So would you rather I not take care of my responsibilities before I go?" she challenged. "In case you forgot, you're not the easiest person to work for. It's taken me a lot of derring-do to put good people in place to handle all of your...demands."

Impossibly fast, he left the desk and moved *impossibly* closer. Temple gave herself a mental kick when she felt herself blinking uncontrollably. *Jaded, huh?* She studied the subtle designs in his tie and recalled her earlier thoughts over the receipt of attention from a gorgeous man.

Jaded or not, Temple could have kissed Ike Melvin when he gave a quick knock and stuck his head just inside her office door.

"Hey? Are we gonna do this?" he called out with a grin on his face.

Relief forced an almost giddy laugh from the back of her throat.

"Sure we are. I've been thinking about this most of the day." Temple edged around Mataeo. She had arranged a pre-tour of sorts with Ike. They'd take an early look at the warehouse before the actual survey expedition.

Mataeo felt his earlier frustration give way to mild humor as he observed Temple's restless behavior. Clearly, she was thrilled by Ike's interruption. Knowing her reaction had everything to do with him, Mataeo felt himself in the clutches of an emotion he couldn't quite label.

"What's up, man?" Ike's voice was a tad labored since he was clearly thrilled by Temple's greeting. "We're takin' a walk through the site before the big day—sort of like a dress rehearsal," he explained, taking part in a hearty shake with Mataeo.

"We should get going, Ike," Temple called from where she was collecting her things off the sofa.

"Why don't you come along, man? We could always use input from the top dog."

Temple froze, her tote hanging at an awkward tilt where it'd paused en route to her shoulder.

Mataeo noticed. Bowing his head, he stroked his jaw and pretended to debate the idea.

"Think I'll pass, Ike. I'm pretty sure you'll be in good hands, though." He strolled around the desk to resume his place along the edge. A grin softened his remarkable features as he watched Temple practically push Ike out the door.

North Shipping's acquisition of the property along Wilmington Harbor was a coup indeed. The under-developed industrial tract along the west bank would make for a prime location—not only for high-density container storage but also for the development of deep-water terminals. Hopes were high that such a location might also allow for increased shipping traffic and cargo volumes.

The much-talked-about survey expedition was at last under way. Mataeo spent the lion's share of his time at the beginning of the event accepting compliments from Yates and his crew. Mataeo took it all in stride as though he were used to it—which he was. North Shipping had made its name a hundred times over as a gutsy company willing to make moves that no one else would dare contemplate.

The recently acquired property had remained in its underused state for years. The previous owner seemed content with the modest profits he gained from the mere storage of a few hundred containers. With North Shipping overseeing the redevelopment for the past few months, vast changes were already evident, hence the accolades from the Yates crew and outrage from the Sanford Norman team.

Temple found an unclaimed spot along the pier and enjoyed a brief moment of solitude. She'd received as many compliments regarding the expedition as Mataeo had. In spite of it all, she felt good knowing that her work for North Shipping would end on a high note.

"Well, well. Congratulations!"

She made a slow turn in the direction of Sanford Norman's voice. "Thanks. We worked really hard to get this to come together." She folded her arms over the plum denim jacket she wore with matching "skinny" jeans and riding boots. She waited, knowing there was more meaning beneath the man's good-natured words.

"You two sure played this one close to the vest." Sanford rested his elbows on the wooden rail lining the pier and focused out over the calm waters. "Nobody had a clue Mataeo was goin' after this land."

"Well, who would have?" Temple leaned against the rail, scanning the purple-orange sky, the lighted warehouse and the guests milling about. "It's not exactly the most beautiful place on the radar."

"Even still." Sanford rose to his full height. "The most ignored place will eventually get attention." He tugged the cuff of the black cotton shirt he wore. "Our friend North doesn't ignore much for long—especially when it *is* the most beautiful place on the radar."

Temple set her head at another angle but did little

else to acknowledge she'd captured Sanford's lurid meaning.

He turned and rested his elbows behind him against the rail. "Noticed you two at Yates's party…on the balcony."

Temple made a move to leave. Sanford blocked her.

"This isn't a road you want to take," she advised, voice soft and gaze calm.

Sanford's laugh sounded more menacing than humorous. "Temple, hon, I'm only *complimenting* Mataeo. He's so used to getting compliments, right? I just thought I'd add a few more to the pot."

"Then I'd suggest you go on and give them in person."

Sanford's green stare turned into more of a leer then. "Honey, I'm only checking to see if you're givin' it up to North because he's your boss or whether any player in the shippin' business will do."

She slapped his face before the last word left his tongue.

Her intention was to leave the event following the scene with Sanford Norman. Unfortunately, Ike found her first. The tour was done and a small cocktail party had been organized along the pier. The evenings were growing a tad chillier so an array of coffees and teas in addition to drinks were available.

Ike was quite pleased by how the expedition had turned out. Temple could tell he'd had his fair share of the bar's alcoholic refreshments. Taking on the role of the Good Samaritan, Temple led Ike by the arm toward the beverages, intending to fill him with coffee.

Though Ike's tongue was understandably loose, given the amount of drink in his system, Temple found his manner more amusing than agitating. Following her "chat" with Sanford Norman, she welcomed Ike's idiotic rambling. Sadly, the evening wasn't about her and her bruised feelings. She knew it wouldn't do well for the rest of their guests to find the North Shipping crew chief so…relaxed. Temple figured it'd be best to get him out of sight. Once Ike was fixed up with a hot cup of coffee, Temple hustled the man back to his office.

In spite of being tipsy, Ike apparently recognized a prime opportunity when he saw one. No sooner had the office door shut behind him did he have Temple in his arms.

"Do you know how long I've thought about taking you out?" His head lolled a bit in the direction of her neck. "Taking you to bed?" he added with a juvenile snicker.

Temple didn't take Ike's words or actions to heart. He was quite obviously drunk and she celebrated her decision to get him off the pier pronto. It was also quite obvious that Ike's drunkenness leaned more in the way of giggling and stumbling instead of more violent behavior. His attempts to pull her close while she led him to his desk were weak, so she found no reason to feel threatened.

Mataeo thought differently. He stormed into the office just as Temple and Ike reached the desk.

"Taeo, what—?"

Mataeo tugged Temple out of his path before she could finish her query. Grabbing Ike by his shirt collar, he prepared to land a blow with the fist he'd cocked.

"Mataeo, wait!" Temple's reflexes kicked in and she caught his arm before it surged. "Wait!" She inhaled deeply and kept his arm tight against her chest. "He's just a little drunk—" Her heart lurched when his gaze fixed on her. "He's only a little drunk, it's fine. I'm fine." She released his arm to curl her fingers into his dark shirt. "I'm fine. I don't need you to do this—not here and definitely not tonight." She watched the rage in his eyes merge into something akin to understanding. She could feel the tension leave his chest where she held his shirt.

Ike had passed out; he dropped to his desk when Mataeo released him. He sat slumped on the corner and it would probably be safe to bet he'd be on the floor in another minute. The situation had Temple caught between mild amusement and heightened frustration. A moment later, she was bolting from the office.

Temple slammed her front door and then slammed a few other doors in her apartment just because she was pissed as hell. She'd been asking herself whether every man on the planet had picked *that* night to lose his mind or if it was simply the men she was *lucky* enough to know.

She studied the bar in the corner of the living room and tapped fingers to her forehead while deciding if she wanted to follow Ike's example and get toasted. Her answer was yes and she'd made it halfway to the well-stocked shelf of beverages when a key scratched in her lock.

Her hands propped on her hips, Temple shook her head as Mataeo entered her home. "I think it's time for you to give that back," she said when his key ring hit the table near the entryway.

He offered no response and Temple left off demanding her house key. She blinked, taking a small step back when he took off his casual jacket and went to work on his shirt.

"Mataeo—" was all she had the chance to say before her mouth was otherwise occupied. Reflexively, she fought against what she wanted.

Mataeo allowed it. That is, he allowed it until his tie was loose, tossed to the sofa and his shirt was unbuttoned and tugged free of his trousers. Then, he took her fists in one hand and squeezed her wrists until the fight left her.

Temple tried again to wrench free once he'd abandoned her mouth to trail his along her throat. He simply gave her another warning tug.

"I can't." Her sob was interlaced with a moan. "I can't do this…."

"*I* can." Gently, he sank his teeth just barely into a soft spot at the base of her throat.

"*I* can't," she persisted.

"Then let me change your mind." He followed the proposal with the force of his mouth on hers.

Chapter 9

The kiss carried on from the living room to the bedroom. Mataeo had been inside her home so often that he had no need to ask for directions or to keep his eyes open while he made his way there during the passionate exchange occurring between them.

Temple toed off her boots and let herself be led. Eagerly, she let herself fall victim to the trembles that ravaged her body. They brought a surge of intense pleasure to every part of her. Inhibition was cast aside and she kissed him wantonly and without regret. With what sounded like a whimper, she thrust her tongue against and around his. She splayed her hands across his broad shoulders and rubbed her covered breasts across his bare chest in an unrelenting show of desire.

She was tossed without ceremony on her bed. She looked around then as though she were coming out of a trance. Before any warnings had the chance to rise up from her subconscious, Mataeo was there, sheltering her with the strength and security of his powerful frame covering her.

Temple felt an unaccustomed purr lilting from her throat. His hands roamed over her arms, locking about her wrists again and drawing them above her head. He nibbled her earlobe without the slightest show of mercy while Temple arched and rotated her hips beneath his. Mataeo breathed her name. His beautifully crafted lips trailed down from Temple's ear to outline her collarbone with the tip of his tongue.

Soon, his gorgeous face was hidden in the lush wealth of her cleavage. Temple gasped at the exquisite feel of him inhaling the scent of her skin. Faintly, those warnings from her subconscious made their presence known again.

"Wait...." She barely managed the whisper.

Mataeo responded by dipping his middle finger into her mouth. He grunted his approval when she suckled it ravenously. Losing whatever resistance he had, he tore into her blouse with no care for the delicate buttons securing it. Then he spent a few wondrous moments outlining her lace-covered breasts with his nose. A firm press released the front clasp of her bra. A second round of outlining commenced then and only the tip of his nose encircled her satiny bare flesh that time.

Temple's mouth parted, but no sound followed. She was way too affected to even make the attempt. Her body curved into a sensual bow, silently pleading that he replace his nose with his mouth. He refused to meet her request and she heard his low chuckle when she sucked her teeth out of frustration.

Mataeo was kind enough to add his fingers back into the mix. Cupping and fondling, he tortured her nipples while his mouth paid homage to the firm coffee-brown skin stretched across her stomach. He plied her navel with a deep kiss and made it deeper still when she cried out.

Temple barely had the time to recover from the navel kiss before Mataeo was treating her mouth to another. Once again, she was drawn in by his tongue dueling playfully over and under her own. She was so mesmerized by the kiss, she paid no mind to the fact that he was slowly pulling her out of her clothes.

Mataeo retraced his journey down Temple's neck and across her collarbone, making a stop to tend to her breasts. Temple clasped her hands around his head to keep him in place as he suckled the tips puckering for his attention. He tended to one in the sweetest, most thorough manner while his fingers took care of its twin.

Temple was oblivious to all else, even the fact that she was nude—which she discovered when his fingers entered her body. She bit her lip on the double caress he subjected her to and brought her hand down over his as he pleasured her.

Mataeo exercised his strength and withdrew. This was the one thing he didn't intend to rush. *Easier said than done,* he realized when she rained soft wet kisses across the rigid chords along his neck.

Impossibly, her arousal elevated when her nails grazed the unyielding plane of his broad chest. Like silk over steel, his skin beckoned her touch. The muscles flexing beneath it beckoned her appraisal. She reached out for him when he moved to slide down before her.

His hands eased under her bottom as if to set her in place for what he had in store.

"Mmm…Taeo…" Temple gasped out when his nose began its maddening journey across her sex. Again, she arched her body, silently urging more appropriate attention.

Mataeo made her wait, of course. His nose brushed the petals framing her femininity and he somehow managed to ignore the way her scent made his shaft swell more than it already had. He felt drained of the desire to do anything but pleasure her and take pleasure from her.

Her hips lifted high off the bed when his tongue plunged deep inside. Mataeo squeezed her thighs while drawing her back down to the tangled covers. Temple's breathing had grown labored. The sound filled the room while she raked her fingers through her hair and quietly begged him not to stop what he was doing to her.

Mataeo wouldn't have dreamed of it. His fingers flexed into her round bottom and he drank more deeply of her. It was as though he was starved for the potent treat that lay at the heart of her body. He had wanted to take his time taking her but knew that he was fast reaching the limits of his willpower. There would be more, he promised himself. There'd be more times, many more. She was his—every bit of her. He was done lying to himself that she had ever been anything less.

Temple opened her eyes when she felt him leave her then.

"What's wrong?" She blinked, propping up a bit on her elbows.

Mataeo didn't answer and didn't need to when he pulled the open shirt off his back. He stood to remove the rest of his clothes. Temple bit her lip as her lashes fluttered at the feel of the liquid need slowly streaming up her thighs in response to the image he cast.

Mataeo checked his trouser pockets and withdrew a few silver packets. Temple swallowed when he tossed them on the bed and she realized there were more than *a few.* Fixed upon her spot in the bed, her mouth went dry as she watched him roll the sheet of latex over his swollen length. Once done, he moved close and Temple raised her head when he silently requested another kiss. He settled between her thighs and they both shuddered as their bodies became one.

Temple's hands were half clenched into fists. Her body was enveloped in a shroud of sensation as Mataeo claimed her with every hard inch of his sex. She moaned into his mouth when his tongue stroked her, steady and deep.

At last his sex was completely hidden inside hers. The strokes from his tongue while he kissed her kept a rhythm with the strokes of his thrusts. Temple didn't think anything could match or top the sensation until he pulled her thigh just slightly away from his body. The move allowed him to increase the depth of the seductive lunges.

Temple took what he gave willingly and without question. How many times had she imagined what this would be like with him? Not even during her most X-rated daydreams had she even come close. She had hoped to be a more giving partner but just then all she could do, all she wanted to do was lay there, take and… enjoy.

Mataeo captured a nipple and suckled it raggedly. He lathered the molasses-dark bud with his tongue and smiled when he felt her coming against the thin sheet of the condom.

"Mataeo… Mmm, I—I'm sorry.…" She apologized in the midst of her climax for not waiting on him to arrive there with her.

Her words had Mataeo giving into the demands of his hormones soon after. He suckled her nipples a bit more harshly, overwrought by pleasure and desire for the woman in his arms.

Gradually, their movements slowed and together they drifted just slightly from their high. Bodies still connected, they fell into an intimate slumber.

Mataeo didn't give Temple time to second-guess a thing that happened between them. Their first encounter that evening was followed by a succession of erotic sessions throughout the night. Afterward, they'd slept soundly.

Temple was first to awaken when the faintest streams of dawn made their way past the edges of her bedroom's bourbon-colored drapes. She found Mataeo sleeping on his stomach, not at all roused by morning encroaching on the serenity of darkness.

Convinced that he dozed too soundly to be easily awakened, Temple treated herself to stroking the powerful line of his shoulders and back. The broad plane was packed with muscle. Temple strummed her nails across the gorgeous honey-doused expanse of it. She imagined the sinews of muscle rippling powerfully as he'd claimed her body so richly and so frequently the night before.

Mataeo shifted on the bed and Temple snatched her hand away. She took a closer look at her bedroom then. There would be no need for doubts or regrets if they could simply remain there.

That wasn't realistic thinking, of course. The world would find a way to intrude and the sheer magnificence of what had gone on there between them would be tarnished.

She'd told Meg that her biggest worry was surviving being cast aside by Mataeo once he'd had his fill. Now there was more.

Sanford Norman would become an even more vicious snake if he lost the deal with Manson Yates. He already knew there was more than business between her and Mataeo. While petty, Temple knew the man would not be above treating his wounds with a healthy dose of public humiliation for the two of them.

It wouldn't take much to make that happen, especially when so many already believed her successful career was a result of time well spent on her back.

She smothered a groan, hiding her face in her hands for a few seconds. When she looked across her bedroom again, resolve illuminated her expression. After pushing back the covers, she eased gingerly from the bed, glancing back repeatedly to see if Mataeo still slept.

She made quick work of tossing things in a few bags. Having enough clothes wouldn't be an issue where she was headed. She slapped on a pair of sweats, tied up her hair and decided to shower and change at Meg's before leaving town.

Temple made one last stop by her bed. Mataeo was sure to be furious when he realized she'd gone. She couldn't worry over that, though. Besides, he'd be busy enough working the Yates deal. In spite of everything, the survey expedition had been a success. Yates and his people had been thoroughly impressed. Mataeo was sure to make the sale, if he hadn't already.

When he shifted in bed again, she figured she'd hesitated long enough and hurried from the room.

Chapter 10

Later that morning, from the comfort of Temple's rumpled bed, Mataeo did in fact close the Yates deal. He'd made an *innocent* call to thank Manson Yates for attending the event. For good measure, he added that he'd hoped it hadn't been a waste of the man's time.

At ten in the morning, Manson Yates was wide awake and full of compliments about the previous evening's festivities. He was also ready to do business with North Shipping. The two made a gentleman's agreement by phone, but Yates wanted to see Mataeo in person later that day to put it all in place.

Beyond pleased, Mataeo clenched a triumphant fist in response to the request. "Thank you, sir. I assure you your client list will be in good hands."

Another satisfied chuckle came through the line from Yates's end. "I've got no doubts about that, son.

We'll meet at my club later today. Let's say around one. That sound good to you?"

"Sounds great, sir. See you then." Keeping his mind on business once the connection broke with Yates, Mataeo searched for another number in his phone. He laughed when Ike Melvin's groggy voice filled the line after five rings.

"Rise 'n shine," Mataeo greeted.

"What? Hell…Taeo? Time is it?"

"Time to get your ass out of bed. We got Yates."

"Mmm? Say what? Yates?" Hungover, Ike was slow to get his bearings.

Mataeo grinned while reaching over to grab the TV remote from the nightstand. "We got the Yates deal. Just talked to him."

"No kidding?"

"No kidding. I need you there with me when we meet him later today."

"Yeah. Yeah, no doubt. I'm there—I'm there— damn."

Mataeo chuckled, well aware that his friend was probably fending off the effects of a bad headache. "You gonna be okay?" His words were mingled with amusement.

"Yeah—yeah, I'll be good." Ike paused to yawn. "Just do me a favor and don't let me order anything but coffee to drink."

"Ha! Deal." Mataeo promised before dissolving into more laughter.

"So did I make a complete ass of myself last night?"

Mataeo settled deeper into the bed and began to surf channels. "Not a *complete* ass."

"Damn," Ike grunted. "You think I screwed up my chances of a date with Temple?"

"Couldn't say." Mataeo made a more serious attempt at silencing his laughter then.

"Damn." Ike took the comment to mean the worst. "Guess I'll give her a call later to find out for sure."

"Well, you may have to wait on a date, anyway. She was holding off on a trip until we settled the deal." Mataeo tossed aside the remote. "For all I know, she's already gone." His smirk was smugness personified when Ike muttered another curse.

"She give second chances?" he asked.

"I doubt it."

"Crap…hell, I'll think of somethin'… Later, much later when my brain's ready to handle thinkin' again."

Mataeo laughed. "Well, we're meeting Yates at his club. One o'clock."

"Got it."

Mataeo left the bed soon after the call with Ike had ended. Though he'd been there countless times, the room held more of his attention that time. Stark naked, he strolled the spacious dwelling. He observed the soft color scheme that struck him more as mellow than feminine.

His vibrant brown gaze narrowed as he smiled. He reached out to graze his fingertips across the various bottles and jars on her dresser. His eyes filled with a sly intensity when they slid toward the walk-in closet. He wouldn't totally invade her privacy by going through her lingerie but since the doors were open…

Mataeo took a peek inside the softly lit area, intrigued by the rows of clothing. One particular row held a line of negligees and housedresses. He rubbed the gauzy material of one piece and couldn't resist bringing it close to inhale her scent. His easy expression tightened somewhat. Thoughts had emerged of her wearing the garment he held for another man.

Mataeo quickly shook off the agitation. He of all people certainly had no right to be angry or even question her private life. Anger and questions filled him just the same. He knew she was regretting last night. He could almost feel it vibrating off her when she had sat down next to him that morning—debating before she left.

He'd let her stew over it awhile. They were, after all, in uncharted territory. Hell, it was territory neither of them had ever planned to explore let alone knew existed. He'd allow her the time it'd take for him to complete the deal with Yates. Then, she was his.

Charleston, South Carolina—Edisto Beach...

Phillip and Aileen Grahame had enjoyed the perks of early retirement and left their native Charleston to move next door to the equally stunning Edisto Island. With its glorious view of the Atlantic, the Grahames had enjoyed several years at their beautiful island home until Phillip's passing three years prior.

The couple's five daughters wouldn't allow their mother an instant of loneliness and the family had remained a close-knit group. The three youngest girls, separated in birth by only a year each, divided their time between home and college in Columbia, South Carolina, and Atlanta, Georgia.

Temple and her twin Tempest were the eldest of the five. Tempest lived in Charleston with her husband of six years, Gregor Hammond. Temple had been the only one of the five to completely pull up roots and relocate.

"Well, how could you just leave like that?"

"Wasn't he as good as he looks?"

"Girl, hush! Of course he's as good as he looks."

Temple only shook her head while going about her unpacking. As her luck would have it, her three baby sisters were home for the next two weeks. Temple had completely forgotten Tempest and Gregor would be celebrating their anniversary at week's end. A huge soiree was already planned.

Helena Grahame threw a pillow at her younger sisters Aliya and Gladys. "Y'all cool it talkin' about Mataeo," she snapped.

Temple turned to catch Aliya in the midst of a shrug. "It's just a long story, all right?"

"And you ain't about to share it with us," Gladys said.

Temple closed her eyes, not even attempting to hide her uneasiness from her sisters. "It's not that, Glad, just…it's just too convoluted to go into right now." She sighed, regretting the girls had overheard (or eavesdropped) on her conversation with their mother when she'd arrived.

Helena cocked her head toward the guest room door and they began making their exit.

"Sorry we butted in, Tem." Helena slapped her hands on the sides of her linen jumper and shrugged. "We know we don't have as much experience as Mama or Tess, but we *are* good listeners."

"Oh, honeys." Temple forgot her weariness and crossed the room to her sisters. "I love you guys." She pulled them into hugs. "Tell Mama I'm gonna take a nap but I'll be down to help with dinner, okay?" she said while stepping out of the embrace.

Alone, Temple strolled out to the balcony overlooking the back of the property. *How could I leave like that?* She repeated Aliya's question.

She'd pissed away a perfect opportunity for them to hash it all out for good. Now they'd creep around what had happened, which would only add to the tension and lessen the chances for them to come out of the entire situation as friends.

Friends, ha! If there was one thing she knew: Mataeo North didn't remain friends with the women he'd quickly loved and let go. She doubted he even started out with them as friends.... Would that make it more or less frustrating for the two of them?

Her cell phone vibrated on the rolltop desk across the room. Temple held her breath while walking toward it, expecting to see Mataeo's name on the caller ID. It was Kendall Ingram.

"Hey!" Relieved she'd answered the call, Temple leaned against the polished desk.

"Hey, yourself. You sound in good spirits. Hope you feel as good when you get down here to—"

"Kendall? I'm here."

"Where?"

"Here. Charleston. My parent's place." She laughed when silence met her words.

"Well, well...what made you up the date?"

Temple traced a swirl in the wood. "I finished up my

business in Wilmington. Since it's T. and Greg's anniversary…"

"That's right. Yeah, the party." Kendall sighed. "I wouldn't miss it. Those two really know how to celebrate being married."

"Yeah, they do…." Temple looked past the balcony again.

"So what's up? You ready to take a look at these places I've got lined up? Or um…has anything changed with you makin' that move?"

"No, Kendall, um…just tell me when and where." Her laughter came easily as Kendall's excitement practically came through the phone line. They spoke a few moments longer before ending the call. Seconds later, the phone buzzed again. It was Tempest.

"Tell me what's going on and don't you dare leave a thing out."

For the first time since she'd gotten up that morning, Temple allowed herself to breathe.

Mataeo was standing behind his desk checking over documents before making his way out to meet with Manson Yates. He checked his wristwatch and was turning for the door when Sanford Norman arrived.

"Congratulations to the business man of the hour!" Sanford greeted him in a tone that could be described as anything but satisfied. "Least Yates had the decency to call and tell me himself." Sanford strolled the office, hands hidden in the pockets of his salt-and-pepper trousers. "He didn't give much of a reason for turning me down. Just said he felt 'North Shippin' was a better fit.'" Sanford tried to imitate Yates's grand Southern drawl. "I'm pretty sure that was *part* of it."

"What's that supposed to mean?" Mataeo decided to play along and help Sanford get to the point he'd really come there to make.

Sanford shrugged, still playing the role of indifference as he walked the office. "Well, I'm sure your *right hand* had a lot to do with it."

"How so?" Mataeo had taken a seat on the edge of his desk and turned to follow Sanford's pace of his office.

"Don't play dumb, North." Sanford smirked. "You had the Yates's deal in the bag the second that old coot met Temple."

Mataeo shifted his gaze toward the desk. "What are you getting at, Norman?" His well-known and best-avoided temper began to show the slightest signs of heating up.

"Oh, don't get me wrong, man." Sanford raised his hands. "I'm not sayin' she did anything...*untoward,* but she was a big part of Yates feeling North was...a better fit."

"Again I ask, 'how so'?"

Sanford rolled his eyes. "Come on, everyone knows that old geezer has a weakness for couples and love and all that sap."

"Well then, if that was the case, you and Regina would be a better fit than me and Temple." Mataeo's smile reflected phony innocence.

"Don't make me laugh! Everybody knows my marriage is in name only. Hell, if me and Regina could've gotten away with it, we'd have brought one of our lovers to that damned dinner party Yates threw." Sanford's green gaze narrowed accusingly. "You did your homework on what would impress Yates most—guess I shouldn't have an issue with that but it still rubs me the wrong way."

"It's business." Mataeo bit out the words and went back to studying the documents on his desk. "Don't beat yourself up because you didn't have the foresight to move on new property."

"Why don't you cut the crap, North?" Sanford bounded across the room, but stopped before he got too close to Mataeo. "Stop treating everybody like they're idiots. How do you expect us to believe Temple Grahame's your trusty assistant in business matters only?"

"She is." The bite to Mataeo's words was more pronounced that time.

Sanford smiled and headed for the door. He let his parting words drift across his shoulder. "Then I guess that was some other guy she was letting ram his tongue down her throat at Yates's party, hmm?"

"Honey, I'm afraid I'm forced to repeat our baby sister's question. Isn't Mataeo North every bit as good as he looks?"

"This isn't funny, Tess."

"You're right." Tempest Hammond sighed and then let silence preface her next words. "It's confusing as hell. I mean, isn't this what you want? What you've always wanted? You've been in love with the guy since college. Ever since the night he saved—"

"Don't. Tess, don't. I dealt with all that and Mataeo and I make a great working team."

"Except half the team is in love with the other half. Deny it, Tem. Deny that in all the years you've been a *team* you haven't stopped loving him."

Temple switched the phone from one sweaty palm to another.

"Well?"

"All right! No. No, I haven't stopped, but I know what Mataeo can be like with women. Exactly how do you think this could work, Tempest? I for one don't think we could have what you and Gregor do."

"And just why not?"

"Doesn't matter." Temple stubbornly refused her twin's question. "I've already made up my mind. I'm quitting. Kendall's gonna come by to help me choose between the places I've narrowed down."

The sound of Tempest sucking her teeth came through the line. "You know, even with all your smarts you still don't have a clue. It's not gonna be nearly as easy to do as you think."

"Yeah, well…" Temple stared absently past the windows. "I can always hope, can't I?"

Chapter 11

Mataeo, along with his business attorney, Eaton Broward, Ike Melvin and others, sat laughing, eating and closing a multibillion-dollar deal with Manson Yates and his team. In truth, the deal had been closed before the entrées arrived. The figures and conditions had already been scoured and *re*scoured by both Mataeo's and Manson Yates's groups when the "deal" was just in its pitching stages. Laughter ran high as did the cigar smoke and conversation among the table of men.

"I was hoping to catch a glimpse of your lovely assistant." Manson leaned over to whisper to Mataeo below the din of raised voices.

"Well, sir, she's not really my assistant." Mataeo smiled, keeping his gaze downcast.

"Hell, kid, that's obvious. Not to mention you first introduced her as your CEO." Manson chuckled and clapped Mataeo's shoulder reassuringly when he looked put out.

Mataeo shook his head then. "What I mean is, she's more like my right arm—closer to a partner. There aren't many of my business decisions that get made without her input."

"I see." Manson sobered a bit. "I could tell that she was a highly intelligent young woman. You're lucky to have her."

"Very." Mataeo accepted the words with a nod yet the expression on his face was obviously tense. "Sir... is my relationship with Temple what fueled your decision to go with North over Sanford's company?"

It was Manson Yates's turn to appear tense. "Sorry that I gave that impression, son. All my reasons for going with North were made on solid business platforms with the exception of one. I just don't like the man." He leaned back and tugged on the crisp cuffs of his suit coat. "I didn't like him as a person and sadly— in business—that can make or break a deal no matter how on top of the game a person is businesswise."

Again Mataeo nodded, considering the older man's words.

"Everyone knows about that sham marriage of his and yet he had the nerve to parade his wife around like they were some happy couple," Manson noted.

"But for not being married, I'm not that much different from Sanford," Mataeo admitted with a shrug. "I'm as much of or maybe even more of a womanizer." He smiled ruefully over his use of the word.

Yates chuckled softly as though he had the inside

scoop on a joke. He took a sip of the bourbon that had been ignored while he conversed with Mataeo.

"Tell me, son. How many of your women have you thought about reaching out to since you settled it in your mind that you're intent on having your lovely… *partner* in your corner for more than business?" Manson didn't wait on a reply, but joined in on another conversation at the table.

Just as well, for Mataeo's mind was completely focused elsewhere.

Temple treated herself to a brief nap in the passenger seat of Kendall's SUV as they made their way back to her mother's place at Edisto Beach. The relaxation radiated up and outward from someplace deep in her soul. Regardless of her reasons for heading home so quickly, she couldn't deny that going home had been the right decision. The trip was very right and very needed. Still, a frown did work its way between the natural arch of her brows when Kendall's voice pulled her from her slumber.

"We're back."

"Sorry, Ken," Temple apologized after inhaling a hearty helping of the sea air.

"Forget it." Kendall reached over to tug the hem of the lightweight blouse she wore with jean capris. "When I saw you, I could tell you were beat. Besides, who could resist submitting to full relaxation out here?"

"That's the truth." Temple eased a coarse lock of hair behind her ear. "But that's not what I'm apologizing for. Sorry I couldn't make a decision—again." She bumped her head against the rest. "I fell in love with all of them, *all* over again."

Kendall chuckled. "It's all right, Tem. They're all gorgeous. You're entitled to be indecisive."

"Maybe. But I know you've got other clients who'd probably make snappier decisions. I'm holding up your progress and your money."

"Stop, that's not it." A grimace tugged at the man's mouth and he stroked his beard to cover it.

"Come on, Ken. I'm a businesswoman. I can take it."

"It's all good, Tem."

"We go back to the sandbox, Ken. Come on."

"Damn. All right, already. I do have someone asking, okay?"

"So go on and show the place then."

"No. I promised you first refusal and I meant that."

"There's no harm in showing the places, Ken."

"True if I'm showin' 'em to *you*. This client may be every Realtor's dream." He flinched and laughed when Temple swatted at his head.

"Okay then, I'll make you a deal." She half turned on the seat. "If I don't make a decision this week, you promise to show the places to your other clients." She tilted her head, attempting to catch a better view of Kendall's face.

"I'll think about it," he said finally, smirking when she pinched his arm. "Well, well." His gaze was focused straight ahead. "Looks like Miss Aileen has company."

Temple turned on the seat. Her easy expression faded when she saw the familiar silver-and-black SUV with North Carolina tags sitting in her mother's driveway.

"No," she whispered.

"What?" Kendall's eyes shifted toward her.

She was already shaking her head. "Nothing." The murmur was barely audible as she left Kendall's vehicle.

Aileen Grahame's girlish laughter reached Temple's ears before she and Kendall even took the first back porch step. Seated at the grand round table in Aileen's pristine kitchen was Mataeo North. He appeared quite content with a tall glass of milk and a fresh batch of Aileen's homemade apple cinnamon cookies on the plate before him.

"Now isn't this fine?" Aileen clapped once and her pale gray eyes sparkled happily. "I feel like one lucky woman to have so many visitors. Get yourself some cookies, Kenny," she ordered after greeting the man with a hug.

Temple noticed Mataeo eyeing Kendall and she made intros before Ken could help himself to the cookies.

"Heard a lot about you," Ken said as he and Mataeo shook hands.

"Wish I could say the same. All I know is you're one hell of a Realtor."

Temple turned her stunned hazel gaze toward the gleaming white linoleum. She wondered what else Mataeo knew. Her heart sank as she heard Kendall cover "what else" quite thoroughly.

"…and trying to get Temple settled into a new place down here," Kendall finished.

A chill shimmied up her spine when Mataeo gave her the benefit of his stare.

"Is that right?" The soft query belied the probing intensity of his eyes.

"She's havin' a dog of a time tryin' to decide."

"Is she now?" Mataeo's warm deep eyes raked Temple's body with new interest. "Well, we can't have that. We'll take another stab at it tomorrow," he declared, daring her to argue.

"So that's settled." Aileen clapped her hands again. "Kendall, baby, I was just about to start dinner. Y'all go on in the living room and relax. I'll be done in two shakes."

"Ah, Miss Aileen, I'd love to but I should hit the road." Kendall's disappointment was genuine. "I don't like the sound of that wind. I better get back to Charleston before dark." He leaned down to kiss the woman's cheek and took the plastic bag of cookies she offered.

"Mataeo." Kendall extended his hand for another shake. "Good meetin' you."

"Lemme show you out, baby." Aileen took Kendall's arm.

Temple prepared to follow. She heard her name before she could take a second step.

"Why'd you leave?" he asked.

"What, Mataeo?" She faced him with agitation in her eyes. "Didn't you have enough?"

He was less than an inch away before she could blink. His hand was on her chin and kept her from looking away.

"Don't you remember I told you I was coming down here?"

"But how much of it has to do with coming to see Miss Aileen and how much of it has to do with us?"

She shook her head. "There is no 'us.'"

His hold slackened and she took the opportunity to put distance between them.

"What happened that night was just…emotions getting out of hand, Taeo. All that battling with Sanford Norman to close the deal. Ike being drunk and bringing up all those—those old memories." She shook her head again, more quickly that time.

"Why didn't you tell me you were looking at places down here?" Mataeo decided to ignore her cryptic reference to the past.

"Dammit, Mataeo, do I have to tell you everything?"

His expression betrayed nothing. "You know how much I dislike being kept in the dark."

"And when does anyone ever dare try that with the great and powerful Mataeo North?"

"So you understand how unwise it would be for you to try it?"

Temple laughed, heartily and genuinely. "Don't even, Mataeo. Not with me. I know you very well. Nothing you say is gonna have me shaking in my shoes."

"Nothing I say, hmm?" He bowed his head and stroked the dimple in his chin.

When Mataeo came close to Temple again, it was to capture her mouth in a deep kiss. Of course, that did a fine job of making her shake in her shoes.

"Wait…." Her soft attempt to dissuade him sounded weaker in the midst of her tongue thrusting helplessly against his.

"Taeo…" she moaned and enjoyed additional moments of entwining her tongue with his. "Mama…she'll be back soon."

Mataeo spent more several seconds delivering his devastating kiss. "You're right," he said after plying her with a softer peck below the earlobe while tugging the hem of her blouse.

Temple watched him stroll back to grab another one of the cookies. She was just slumping back against the counter and trying to catch her breath when more familiar voices caught her ear. She cursed low at the sound of her little sisters on their way to the kitchen.

The resulting screams when the young women found Mataeo in the kitchen sent a sharp pain lancing through the back of Temple's skull. The girls practically tackled him with a simultaneous bear hug before stepping back to hug one at a time along with kisses to the cheek. Of course, an array of giggles laced the entire event. Helena, Aliya and Gladys began talking in unison. Each girl wanted to know how long Mataeo would be there, if he was staying with them and if he was at *least* going to stay for dinner.

In spite of her mood, Temple had to take time to observe Mataeo with her sisters. He gave them each the full benefit of his attention and Temple knew they felt like the center of his world when he spoke. His alluring chocolate stare was focused and soft. His voice was deep and soothing. No wonder his success with women was so envied. He had the uncommon ability to make one feel like she was…well, the *only* one.

Temple was coming out of her pensive state in time to hear Gladys ask again whether Mataeo was going to stay with them.

"Well, Miss Aileen already put my stuff upstairs,

but—" he looked toward Temple and nodded once in her direction "—if it isn't all right with your sister…"

Aliya laughed. "What's *she* got to do with it? It's Mama's house."

"On that note," Temple groaned and headed away from the kitchen as new conversation stirred behind her back. She'd hardly cleared the entryway when she heard Mataeo's rumbling chuckle mingling with the girl's giggles.

Temple went in search of her mother, knowing the woman was probably off somewhere dusting her already spotless home. Sure enough, she found Aileen at the end of the long corridor where her room was.

Aileen was busy dusting the other guest room. It didn't take long for Temple to realize her mother had placed Mataeo on the long remote corridor in the room right next to hers.

Aileen waved the dust cloth when she noticed Temple in the doorway. "I'll be down to start dinner in a minute, baby. I just wanted to spruce up in here a bit."

"Mama…" Temple stepped into the room and pushed the white oak door shut behind her. "What are you up to?"

"Honey…" Aileen laughed softly. "Dusting."

Temple closed her eyes.

"Ah, baby, it's all right. Y'all are both adults."

Temple wilted. "Don't I know it," she lamented and settled down to the edge of the king bed in the corner of the room.

Aileen took pity. She balled the dust rag in her hand and went to join her daughter on the bed. "Baby, you know that boy's in love with you."

"A lot of boys have been in love with me, Mama, and you never gave any of 'em a room right next door."

Aileen shrugged, her full lips curving into a girlish pout. "Maybe I would have had you been in love with any of 'em."

Temple opened her mouth to gasp, but no sound emerged.

"Don't you dare try denying it." Aileen slapped Temple's knee. "It's written all over you, you poor thing." She cast a knowing look toward the bedroom door. "If it makes you feel any better, that gorgeous thing down at my breakfast table looks even more pitiful than you do."

With those words, Aileen kissed her daughter's cheek and left her alone.

Mataeo hummed a low, unnameable tune while he unpacked a half hour later. He'd finished putting away his socks and turned, from the dresser, to find Temple outside in the hall.

"If you've got any respect for my parents' house, you'll leave," she told him, and then turned on her heel and walked away.

Mataeo followed Temple to her room and shut the door. "What's that supposed to mean?"

"You're up to no good." She planted her hands on her hips while delivering the accusation.

Mataeo had the decency to agree. "Most definitely. But, since I've got Miss Aileen's blessing, I don't feel nearly as bad about it as I probably should."

"Liar."

Mataeo shrugged and folded his arms over his lightweight sweatshirt. "You could ask her yourself. I told her what my intentions were when I got here."

Temple rolled her eyes. There was no need for confirmation; she already knew where her mother's loyalty resided. Instead, she settled on her bed and fixed him with weary eyes.

"Taeo, this is crazy."

He sat close and trailed his fingers along the length of her thigh. "Can I ask you something?"

She wouldn't respond.

"Did you enjoy what happened between us the other night?"

Again, Temple refused to respond. She did wilt, though, and quite noticeably.

Her reaction was enough to set Mataeo's mouth into a knowing smile as he took note.

Temple recovered quickly and braced herself against his touch along her thigh. "It can't happen again. It would just stir up too much drama."

"And just what do you think pretending it didn't happen will stir up?" He brought his elbows to his knees when she left the bed.

Temple went to stand before the windows. She'd dimmed the lighting in her room in order to take in the view of the beach. Mataeo came to stand behind her and the view was forgotten.

His persuasive, perfectly sculpted mouth brushed her nape, bared by the tousled ponytail she wore. One hand disappeared into the blouse she wore. He unfastened her button fly in tandem with the buttons along her shirt. Temple could have slid down the length of the window then. His touch weakened her that quickly... that thoroughly.

"Ask me to stop." He spoke against her ear while his fingers dipped inside her. They met with a wealth of moisture.

Temple merely shifted her legs and arched her breast against his palm. She whimpered, taking great pleasure in the feel of her nipple grazing the rough center of his hand.

"Ask me to stop." His demand was delivered more firmly that time. For added emphasis, he plied her neck with wetter more insistent kisses. His middle finger thrust higher. She'd barely slid up and down upon it once before he broke contact, kissed her cheek and left the room.

Chapter 12

"Well, y'all are just like two peas in a pod!"

Mataeo arrived downstairs early the next morning only to have Aileen Grahame tell him he and Temple were her only two guests up at the crack of dawn.

"My three sleeping beauties—" Aileen turned her gaze toward the ceiling "—are still dead to the world. Can I fix you some breakfast, sugar?"

"Thanks, Miss Aileen." Mataeo didn't mask the curiosity in his eyes as he scanned the sunlit kitchen. "Temple eat already?"

"Oh, she's out hanging clothes," Aileen called from the refrigerator.

"Don't know why I'm surprised," Mataeo said after he'd allowed disbelief to show on his face for a scant moment.

Aileen was laughing as she pulled juice from the refrigerator. "Never cared much for cookin' my clothes in a dryer, sugar."

Ten minutes later, Aileen had supplied Mataeo with a basket of juice, biscuits and salmon croquettes and pointed him in the direction of where he could find Temple.

Mataeo enjoyed the walk toward the edge of the property overlooking the beach. He could see why she'd want to be there but that didn't mean he had to accept her decision to leave. He knew that's what she was planning. He supposed a part of him had known it all along. She needed to leave even more so now following their… encounter.

Grimacing then, he shifted the basket to his other hand. They were most certainly in a mess which was usually the outcome once sex was added to the mix. Then again, sex, or some aspect of it, had been part of their relationship from the jump, hadn't it?

His hand tightened on the basket and his skin felt heated in spite of the T-shirt he wore with his dark nylon sweats. Even after all these years, that incident still had the power to turn him livid.

He saw her in the distance—the wind was making the clothesline ripple as she attempted to hang the clothes that filled the basket at her feet.

The fierce breeze stirred Temple's housedress, causing the multicolored material to flare around her calves. Mataeo stopped moving toward her and relished the sight of her drawing her hair back into a neater ponytail. She went back to work on the clothes, having no idea of the effect she had on him.

All this time she'd been right there before him,

Mataeo thought. Taking things to the level they had now reached had never once occurred to him.

Perhaps they would have, had things not started between them in such a dangerous manner. It was a manner that could have been more dangerous for Temple had he not shown up when he did. Girls like her were prime targets on a college campus. Good girls from good families. Girls who didn't do unseemly things or hang out with unseemly characters. The phrase *unseemly characters* was a good description of himself in those days. He'd only had a few classes with Temple but that was enough to tell him she was sweet, smart, special and trusting. Too trusting.

He'd stopped the idiot minutes after the guy had trapped her on the front seat of his car and ripped open her shirt. A date gone bad in the worst possible way, Mataeo recalled. His mouth twisted harshly as images of the incident filtered through his mind as clearly as the night it'd happened.

Temple hadn't been fully violated but the damage had been done just the same. That sweet, trusting element had dimmed. She had become smarter because of what happened but damaged just the same. In the days following, she clung to him and their friendship began primarily because of her fear.

He could see in Temple's eyes that he was more protector than friend. That had been okay with him. Protecting her, whether she needed him to or not, had become his purpose.

Now that purpose had diluted with desire and…love? Well…yes, he'd always loved her, but somehow without him being aware of it that love had raised above the platonic level and into that more potent realm.

The grimace commanding his expression slowly gave way to a smile that softened his magnificent features. Mataeo continued on his path toward her. No way in hell would she ever buy that he loved her. In lust, yes—love? Not Mataeo North—a guy who'd saved himself, raised himself, scraped his way through school, become a definite success and viewed women as toys he couldn't get enough of. Temple had been witness to his "playa" persona for years and now he expected her to believe he'd changed? Who the hell was he fooling?

Temple jumped and her hands tightened on the clothesline, causing it to vibrate noticeably. Surprise beamed on her lovely face when she saw Mataeo leading down to where she was.

The line was fashioned between two towering moss trees. It was her favorite place to hide out, to enjoy a book or a nap once the chore of hanging clothes was done. In a family of five girls, hiding places were essential.

Mataeo read the question in her light eyes and lifted the basket before she could ask what he was doing there.

"Miss Aileen sent me down with breakfast." He grinned when she continued to watch him warily. "Your staff would have a fit if they saw you out here hangin' clothes."

Temple couldn't help but smile even as she rolled her eyes toward the clothes basket. "Mama doesn't care about me being a business diva." She shrugged. "To her, I'll always be the resident clothes hanger."

"So what's in there?" she asked once their laughter had settled. She motioned to the basket Mataeo brought down with him.

"Let's see…." He knelt to pull out the contents. "Salmon croquettes, I think, and biscuits…." He unpacked the items and set them out beneath one of the huge trees.

Temple had lost track of his words, preferring to focus on the flex of his biceps beneath the short sleeves of the T-shirt he wore. It wasn't hard to notice the man was built like a tank. Of course, the three-piece suits he usually wore didn't offer as many appealing glimpses of the chiseled frame somewhat bared to her gaze just then.

"Temp?"

She blinked and cleared her throat. She'd been staring, and she silently ordered her head out of the swamp. Besides, this wasn't the time or the place to think of sex. Unfortunately, it was all she could focus on since it had first happened between them.

"So congrats on closing the deal." The words came out more abruptly than she would have liked but business talk was by far the safest conversation piece.

"Thanks." He finished unpacking the basket and set it aside. "You were gone when I woke up so I took a chance on calling Yates before I got out of bed." He didn't bother to look back at her but smiled, anyway. He could easily hear the moan she uttered while hanging the last of the clothes.

Temple hesitated after setting the final clothespin

in place. The purpose was to settle her nerves which were now perched on the teetering edge. The attempt was all for nothing when Mataeo came up behind her. She jumped when he took her elbow and led her from the line.

"You should eat." He took her to the shelter of the trees and tugged until she'd followed him down to the pallet he'd set out.

"You didn't have to do all this." She managed a weak smile. "I was coming back to the house as soon as I was done here." She looked toward the line.

"Right." Mataeo slanted a challenging glare in her direction, then waved the book she'd set against the base of the tree. "It's just about the food, Temp." He assured her and smiled when she got comfortable on the pallet.

The wind in the trees offered the most sound then. Silence resided between Mataeo and Temple. Mataeo poured the juice and was handing her the cup when he finally decided to speak.

"Are you afraid of me, Temp?"

Her hand froze over his as she reached out for the cup. "Mataeo…" she breathed and swallowed with great effort. "I can't— I could never be afraid of you."

The response did nothing for his darkening mood. "I'm not asking if you're afraid of me as a friend or as a…protector." He rolled his eyes on the use of the word, and then glared at her once again. "I'm asking if you're afraid of me as a lover."

Temple drank deeply of her juice and prayed her voice would be available when she chose to use it. "What just happened between us has got us confused."

She set aside the cup and began wringing her hands. "It's like I said before. We—we gave into the pressure of tension, business…."

"Hell, Temple, this is a simple question." He covered her hands with one of his. "Are you afraid to let me into your bed again?"

"Why shouldn't I be?" She snatched her hands away. "You don't keep any woman. You're interested up until they sleep with you, which is usually within a few days of them meeting you." She muttered a curse. "I think they only wait *that* long so you won't lose respect for them, which you inevitably do. Then *I* wind up screening their calls to you until they get the hint that you're done with them."

"Christ, Temple…" Mataeo drew up his legs to rest his arms across his knees. "I forgot how well you know me."

"It's the only thing stopping me from making an even bigger fool of myself and sleeping with you again." She almost laughed.

Mataeo smoothed both hands across his soft hair for several minutes before fixing her with another challenging stare. "Doesn't the fact that I want to sleep with you again disprove what you just said about my being interested only until I get what I'm after?"

Her smile came through fully. "I guess you're just making up for lost time." She reached for a biscuit.

Mataeo left the pallet, not bothering to hide his temper.

"Sorry, Taeo." She picked a corner off the flaky biscuit and chewed thoughtfully. "Guess if you'd known this would happen between us, you wouldn't have shared so much of your *game* with me."

"Do you love me, Temple?"

"What?" She dropped the biscuit. Her voice wavered on the one word she spoke.

Mataeo faced her but he wouldn't repeat his question.

Temple moved to her knees and began packing the mostly untouched food in the basket. "Of course I love you. We've been friends since—" She quieted when he dropped down to the pallet and shoved aside the basket.

"I'm not talkin' friends and you damn well know it." He'd taken her arm.

She let him see the tears glistening in her hazel eyes. "Why are you doing this? Can't you just forget that we ever gave into this craziness and go back to what we had?"

"Do you love me, Temp?"

"All right!" She wrenched out of his hold. "What do you want from me, Taeo? What? You want to hear me tell you that I've been suffering in silence since college? That I've loved you ever since the night you saved me from that son of a bitch? That watching you all these years with all your—your *friends* has been killing me?"

Mataeo was frowning. Not in anger, but in discovery. It was as though he was not only *seeing* her for the first time, but understanding. At last, understanding.

"Dammit." Temple's voice was hushed and she turned away as the tears sprinkled her cheeks. "What does knowing all that solve? You're still who you are."

The breeze blew noisily between them for several seconds.

"I swear that I'm not out to hurt you, Temp." He reached out to touch her but resisted. "I know what I am, but as far as I'm concerned, all bets are off now. I've got no comparison to this."

Temple's laughter then was a mix of heartache and amusement. "Are you trying to say that I'm different?"

Mataeo chuckled then, as well. The gorgeous depths of his mocha stare were soft yet probing. He leaned close to press a quick heated kiss on her shoulder. "Yes, love," he admitted.

Temple remained seated and watched him walk away.

Temple savored the solitude of the tree for an hour longer and then she headed back to the house. The place had livened up quite a bit during her absence. The girls were up and bustling about—bustling about Mataeo more accurately.

"How do you take your coffee, Mataeo?" Gladys asked as she hovered near him at the table.

Aliya was near the buffet preparing the man a plate teeming with grits, bacon and eggs. Helena had the remote in hand and was asking if anyone knew what channel was ESPN.

"Oh, hey, Tem," Helena absently greeted her sister.

"The girls were kind enough to offer me breakfast," Mataeo explained once Gladys and Helena welcomed their sister. "Since I didn't get the chance to eat what Miss Aileen fixed."

"Yeah, too bad the wind knocked over the basket," Helena noted.

Temple exchanged looks with Mataeo and nodded over the lie.

"There's enough for you to eat, too, Tem," Aliya offered.

"That's okay, Al. I'm just gonna—"

"Is that somebody turnin' down food?" Tempest Hammond called out as she arrived in the kitchen with her husband, Gregor.

The younger girls practically screamed themselves to pieces at the sight of their brother-in-law. Needless to say, they were ecstatic over the chance to bustle about for two men. Tempest had the chance to hug Mataeo while Gladys, Aliya and Helena tugged Gregor into a seat at the round table.

"I hope you're staying awhile." Tempest cast a sly look toward her husband. "The girls need someone else besides Greg to lavish all their considerable attention on."

"Aw, Tess." Gladys waved off her sister while everyone else laughed.

While Mataeo and Gregor shook hands and caught up, the twins shared a warm, lengthy hug. Though identical, subtle differences in appearance made it a tad easier to tell the two beauties apart. Temple had never cut her hair, while Tempest opted to wear her thick locks in a chin-length style. When she wasn't required to dress in confining business attire, Temple preferred flowing housedresses, sweats and oversize tees. Tempest had a flair for more revealing outfits to flatter her enviable hourglass frame.

"So? How are things?" Tempest inquired amidst the rumble of various conversations filling the kitchen.

Temple toyed with the tassels of her sister's snug burgundy T-shirt. "I told him I loved him and for how long."

Tempest gasped happily and clutched her hands in a show of pure glee.

"Don't get carried away, Tess." Temple studied Mataeo across the kitchen with Gregor. "This won't turn out the way you're hoping."

"Well, I have a feeling my hopes and Mataeo's are one and the same." Tempest studied Mataeo awhile as well before casting a speculative eye upon her twin. "Look, girl, I know you can hold your own with the man, but for how long?"

Before Temple could open her mouth to answer, her sister had whirled away.

"Mataeo, me and Greg expect you to be there for our anniversary party!" Tempest announced.

"Wouldn't miss it!" Mataeo grinned devilishly.

Temple only rolled her eyes when Tempest fixed her with a broad smile.

Chapter 13

Temple decided to spend the day with her sisters while Mataeo enjoyed a guy's day with Gregor. She set out early the following morning to take yet another look at the properties she hoped to choose between before her week's deadline was up. Kendall would soon be showing the places to other clients.

Temple kept her viewing to one place per day. She hoped the extra time spent at each site would help her to decide—finally.

Her smile appeared the moment she opened the door. Nostrils flaring, she took in the inviting aroma that greeted her when she walked into the house on Edisto Island. There wasn't a direct view of the ocean, but the place carried a distinct charm with the trees and brush that sheltered it from view.

"Ken?" Temple figured her Realtor was responsible

for the added aroma therapy touches. *Who knows?* she thought. Maybe it *would* help her choose, she mused.

She hadn't noticed Kendall's SUV out front, but she called out to him while strolling through the house. Its floor plan gave the place an airy, rejuvenating appeal. Equally appealing were the gleaming hardwoods and the loft-style master bedroom suite, which was located right above the cozy den on the main floor.

From there, Temple could tell that the room appeared to be furnished. It hadn't been that way on her last visit.

"Kendall?" Her tone sounded a bit more cautious that time as she made her way up to the bedroom.

Temple's gasp was muted by the hand she threw over her mouth. The room had definitely been furnished. Plum-colored drapes had even been fashioned over the windows. The area would have been bathed in darkness were it not for the weak light drifting up from the den. There was a golden gleam from the electric candles spaced throughout the area.

"Ken?" Temple didn't expect an answer then. She actually preferred no response and decided against further investigation at that point.

She turned to head back but found her way blocked by a solid wall of muscle. Temple backed away from Mataeo, only stopping when she bumped into the inviting queen-size bed. It was already turned down and welcoming occupants.

"Not here, Mataeo," she whispered as he advanced.

"No choice." His ocean-deep voice was almost as soft as hers. "Kendall told me to do whatever I could to help you make a decision."

"Not this way." She swallowed, closing her eyes as

anticipation had its way with her hormones. "This isn't the way, Taeo...." She trailed off once his hands were spanning her waist.

Mataeo was nibbling her earlobe and intermittently trailing his nose along her neck. "Can you think of something better?" he asked her.

Lashes fluttering and moans on the horizon, Temple latched onto whatever excuses she could find. "Kendall's probably coming...on his way back any minute to—to show the place...."

Mataeo made no attempt to halt his assault on her earlobe. His tongue and perfect teeth proved to be a devastating duo as they worked magic on her weakening defenses. His strong fingers strummed a provocative tune along her spine when they ventured beneath the black cap sleeved T-shirt she wore with khaki shorts.

"I don't think he'll be here anytime soon since you've got the place to yourself for the day."

"How? How do you know that?" Her voice intermingled with a moan.

"Kendall's just full of information." His hands raised to cup her breasts, thumbs stroked her nipples simultaneously. "Like I said, he told me to help you any way I could."

"Mataeo, just...mmm...wait...." Her forehead fell against his chest then.

His fingers had already disappeared inside her shorts, inside...her.... Desperate for the climax she'd craved since he'd arrived, Temple clutched his shirt and silently prayed that he would not stop.

Mataeo wouldn't have dreamed of it. He was starved

for her to the point of madness. Heaven help her if she should demand that he stop. He didn't know whether he possessed the slightest bit of will to do so.

"Taeo...don't." She grabbed his wrist when he appeared to be withdrawing. "Put your fingers back inside me...please...." She bit her lip when he obliged.

Mataeo's striking smile emerged in response to her honesty. He knew it was brought on by a healthy dose of arousal. In one lithe move, he gathered her close and settled her on the center of the bed. Temple's shorts and top were memories moments after he placed her there.

When she tried to pull him out of the denim shirt he wore with sagging denim shorts, Mataeo made it clear that he wasn't ready to lose them just then. Linking his fingers through hers, he kept her hands on the covers and brought his mouth down on hers.

Temple was an enthusiastic participant in the act. Her head lifted off the pillows as her tongue fought a provocative battle with his. She wasn't even aware that he'd released her hands until the kiss broke and his mouth worked its way down her half-clothed and trembling body.

Mataeo tortured her nipples, tending to them through the lacy barrier of her bra. His nose encircled a protruding bud before his lips closed over it, treating the tip to the slightest suckling.

"Mataeo...please...please?" She curved her hands about his head in hopes of persuading him to do more. When that indirect encouragement proved useless, she moved to tug down her bra straps. Her hands went weak when he suckled harder.

Greedily, Temple pushed more of herself into his

mouth. She was still writing and arching when Mataeo smoothly unhooked the garment's fastening. Barely a second passed before his lips and tongue were favoring a bare nipple.

Temple shuddered from the need snaking through her. The suckling had turned ravenous. Mataeo switched his attention from one breast to the other. Powerful hands slid beneath her shoulder blades where he pressed and brought her closer to him.

It wasn't enough. Temple wanted so much more and thrust against him insistently and repeatedly. Again, she tugged at the waist of his shorts. When he tried to stop her, she emerged the victor, wrenching her wrists out of his grasp. Determination illuminated her beautiful dark face as she tugged the shorts until the snap gave.

Mataeo kissed his way up to her ear. "I want this to last," he told her.

Temple ignored the tortured words and went to work on his belt and zipper. She felt a measure of tension leave his body as though he'd given up trying to hold out against her. She took him in her hand, working his shaft while nibbling his jaw.

The tiny moans she uttered broke down whatever resolve he had left. He moved above her, pulling the shirt from his back. The shoes he wore had been kicked to the floor long ago and were followed by his shorts and boxers, minus the condom packages he'd pulled from the back pockets.

His interest wasn't in applying protection, but in ripping off what was left of her underthings and returning to feast on her nipples. An unreadable sound settled in the depths of his chest as he lost himself in the fragrant valley between her breasts. He could feel Temple setting the condom in place slowly, intensifying his pleasure in the process.

She'd just eased it into place when he took her. Temple cried out unashamed. Those shudders of pleasure that had overcome her their first time together returned in full force. Temple matched him move for move. She pounded his back with a weak fist when he repeatedly hit the spot that made her whimper. She clutched his ass to ensure he didn't veer from where she wanted him.

"Temple…" Mataeo cupped one breast and flicked his thumb across the nipple while he bathed the other with his tongue. "Temp…" he chanted during the ragged suckling. He rolled to his back and took her with him. He kept his mouth on her while squeezing her full bottom and directing her moves on his wide, rigid shaft.

Sheltered behind the curtain of Temple's thick hair, they were uninhibited. Cries and groans charged the air. Temple pushed herself into a straighter position. She tugged Mataeo's hands from her hips to her chest and held them there as she rode him.

Mataeo squeezed his eyes shut, wincing as he tried to hold out against the exquisite pain that seized him.

Temple released his hands to drag her own through her hair.

Mataeo squeezed her bottom with intentions of stilling her sultry rotations on his sex. He was fast approaching the point of eruption.

"No, please," she sobbed. "Please don't pull me off, not yet…"

The plea was his undoing and he was spewing the proof of his desire some seconds later. When Temple collapsed, as well, Mataeo kept her sheltered against his chest. He brushed his mouth across her forehead until they both drifted off.

"Well, Jenny, we've been seeing a huge surge in gusty winds these past days. That'll continue well beyond this weekend as we keep our eye on that tropical depression just off the coast of Cuba. Right now, it could go either way. Of course, we hope it'll go the *other* way. At any rate, we can expect an increase in clouds, more overcast days and more chance for rain near the end of the week. On a better note, we will have relief from the high temps we've been experiencing over—"

"Mataeo? Can I talk to you?" Temple interrupted the weather report.

"Aw, Tem, we're just about to start the movie," Gladys whined from where she was kneeling next to the DVD player.

"If he misses the beginning, he's gonna be lost." Aliya added her opinion while frowning at her big sister.

Temple somehow produced a smile. "I promise not to keep him long."

"Girls—" Mataeo pushed off the sofa "—don't start it without me and I'll bring more popcorn."

Of course, the young women needed no bribing and were pleased to do as Mataeo had asked them. With a cool wave, he urged Temple to precede him from the den. Silently, he followed her to the cluttered office/library at the end of the long corridor just off from the front door.

"Don't expect an 'I'm sorry' for earlier today," he told Temple the second she closed the door.

She brought her hands to her hips.

Mataeo shrugged. "If that's what you brought me in here to do."

"No, no, Mataeo." Temple smoothed her hands across the seat of her cuffed jeans. "I don't expect you to apologize, especially when you're not the one acting out of character."

"Temp—"

"Do you remember yesterday morning—out at the trees? You told me you didn't have a comparison to what's happening with us?"

Mataeo nodded and took a spot on the arm of the worn leather sofa.

"That's not quite right 'cause when it's all said and done, I'm giving you exactly what you always get— another willing participant in your bed."

His grin was danger and sensuality perfectly blended. "You haven't been in my bed yet, Temple."

She wasn't amused. "I can't be one of your…that whenever, wherever, whatever you get from them can't work with me." She shrugged. "I want more. I…I deserve more and you can't expect me to believe you're ready for that." She waited for some sort of response then, but there was none.

"You can't just snap your fingers and expect me to

drop," she started to ramble. "You can't expect me to be ready for whatever *you* want. I'm not built like that."

Mataeo studied his hands, rubbing one over the other. "So you're saying that you won't sleep with me again?"

Her cheeks burned. "I'm asking you not to do what you did this morning."

"You—"

"I enjoyed it, yes. God, yes." She sighed and walked over to study the back lawn from the windows. "Sooner or later that enjoyment's gonna land me in the same category as your other castoffs."

Finally, Mataeo stood. Shoving his hands deep into the pockets of his loose-fitting jeans, he closed some of the distance between them. "Can't you grasp that you're in no danger of winding up in that category?"

She turned to face him with accusation in her hazel glare. "You can't promise that."

"No." He ran a hand across his head and frowned over the fact. "I've got a lot more work to do. I accept that. You know pretty much all there is to know about me." He grinned, focusing on a weak stream of sunlight across the worn carpet. "You know way too much about the parts of me I'm not so proud of. And there's no game I can pull that you haven't seen me play already."

A measure of amusement came through and Temple let him see her rueful smile. "Guess that's the challenge then, huh? You've got to come up with a new game— then it'd be over." She rolled her eyes when his laughter rumbled into the air.

He moved close and traced his fingers across her

cheek. "What makes you think it'd ever be over?" He kissed her before she could remark or resist.

Resistance was nowhere on the radar, and Mataeo growled his appreciation when Temple responded with little coaxing. Satisfied by her level of participation, he broke the kiss midthrust, his tongue against hers. He nodded slowly then, taking measure of the expression she wore. Clearly, she was quietly ridiculing herself.

"Nobody made a rule saying you can't treat yourself to this, Temp." He nuzzled the curve of her jaw with the tip of his nose. "It's what makes the game worth playing."

Temple shook her head. The movement was fueled by regret. "Some of us have more to lose than others." Her lashes settled slowly over her eyes as his touch threatened to render her speechless. "Some of us get put in terrible positions when we give into enjoyment."

"Do you remember what else I said when we were out there near the trees?" He waited for her eyes to meet his. "I told you I wasn't out to hurt you. We've been friends too long and just the thought of doing that makes me sick." He searched her light eyes with his warm cocoa ones. "I better get back for the movie."

He left the office door open when he walked out. Temple followed into the hall and watched as he strolled away.

Chapter 14

The second property was a gorgeous place on Edisto Beach and not too far from Aileen Grahame's home. Though it was beautiful, with bay windows and balconies that offered the most incredible Atlantic views, it appealed most to Temple because of its closeness to her mother's place.

Mataeo was obviously thinking the same thing. He mentioned it while they took in the view from the screened back porch.

"So I guess Kendall wasn't helping Miss Aileen with property issues, right?"

Temple shoved her hands into the pockets of her gold shirtdress. "How long have you been in the habit of double-checking everything I tell you?"

"I didn't have to double-check on that." He shifted his weight, but didn't look away from the ocean. "I knew it was a lie the second I heard it." He stroked his dimpled chin and looked down then. "I do admit to having Kendall checked out, though. It didn't take much to find out he was helping you with finding places, and since there's nothing wrong with buying property I'd be interested in knowing why you thought you had to lie to me about it."

Temple's laughter carried on the breeze. She took a seat on the top porch step. "Maybe I wanted this to be one of the few things I handled on my own. Something I could look at as my own and not yet another lavish gift from my generous boss."

Mataeo tilted his head and gave her the full benefit of his gaze. "You have a problem with me showing appreciation?"

"I don't have a problem with it." Temple braced her elbows on her knees and bridged her fingers. "Then again, I *do* have the advantage of knowing what they mean."

"Unlike others who might…misinterpret."

"Hmph. Unlike others who *do* misinterpret."

"Has that been a problem for you?"

Temple stood. She glared in Mataeo's direction before heading on down to the beach.

A heavy downpour made its presence known before Mataeo and Temple left the second property. The rain was so blinding it ruled out any thoughts of driving. Temple was soaked by the time she'd raced back after the forty minutes she'd spent at the beach. Of course, there was nothing for her to dry off with when she got back to the house. Mataeo had graciously started a fire.

"This is to die for," Temple said through chattering

teeth as she turned herself before the flames. "I just hope Kendall doesn't give us grief over it."

"I wouldn't worry about it." He used a long, thick stick to stoke the flames. "Can't have you freezin' to death and you need to get out of your clothes. Everything, Temp."

She didn't oblige. "No way am I sitting on the floor naked. Even if there *is* a fire."

"Do what I say, please." He finished with the fire and turned for the front door. "I've got something in the truck you can use."

"What? Newspaper?" Temple knew very well how pristine the man kept his vehicles. No towels or old shirts would be found lying around that could serve her any purpose.

When Mataeo returned with a blanket, Temple couldn't even attempt to hide her surprise.

"You wouldn't have anything to eat out there, would you?" she asked him.

Mataeo shrugged, squeezing water from the tails of the black shirt he wore over a white T-shirt and shaking the blanket he'd managed to keep dry during the brief trip from his SUV. "A blanket's the best I can do since you told me not to do what I did yesterday. Otherwise—" he crossed the glistening hardwoods to where she stood near the fire "—I'd have had the cabinets stocked, towels in the bathroom…." He reached for her hand and absently stroked her palm. "And a bed— already turned down."

Temple didn't know if it was the dampness of her skin or his touch that made her shiver.

"I'm sure the blanket'll be fine until my clothes dry."

She put space between them but didn't move too far from the flames as she awkwardly removed her clothing under the shelter of the blanket.

Mataeo went to peer out at the weather. The rain was still bearing down. Thunder and lightning had been added to the mixture. He looked back to find Temple sitting and shivering against one of the white stone columns in the living room. Muttering an obscenity below his breath, he shut the door and went to her.

Temple inched over to make room when Mataeo returned to sit next to her. She believed he'd wanted to share the column. Her heart made a dancer's leap to her throat when she realized he was peeling back the blanket she was trembling beneath.

"You're gonna catch your death freezing here on the floor," he said when she opened her mouth to argue.

"The fire's warm enough." She nodded toward the towering hearth.

"I can do better than that." He kissed her when her lips parted again.

Temple's verbal response was smothered beneath the kiss. Mataeo took advantage and added his fingers to the spontaneous love play. Temple's fists curved weakly against his massive chest, which was half-visible beneath his damp shirt. His fingers deep inside her were far more heat inducing than the flames raging in the fireplace.

Mataeo rose up, urging Temple to her back. The blanket spread out around her and her body became riddled with goose bumps. Her mind didn't register the chill. Mataeo ended the kiss by trailing his tongue across the even ridge of her teeth and then outlining the full curve of her lips. His mouth grazed down her neck then onto the rise of her bosom. Seconds later, his persuasive kiss was causing Temple to tremble anew. He feasted on her chilled nipples, heating them instantly inside his mouth.

His fingers continued to thrust and rotate inside her. Temple circled herself upon them and she groaned along with Mataeo when her slick need coated his skin. She almost sobbed when he withdrew. She was still arching upward on the lingering sensation of him when his tongue replaced his fingers.

Her hips left the floor only to be set down and held in place when Mataeo squeezed her waist and plunged his tongue deeper—more intensely. Temple reached the verge of orgasm countless times only to have him end the oral treat and torture her with his nose outlining the folds of her sex.

His tongue probed shamelessly, driving high inside her and then withdrawing to flick playfully at the puckered flesh that sheltered her core. Mataeo seemed intent on driving her mad. When he withdrew yet again, it was to suck her clit. His attention to the hypersensitive bud of desire had her practically screaming out her pleasure.

Temple was near tears when he finally showed mercy and took her with his tongue until she climaxed....

Later, the rain had subsided but the clouds remained. With the onset of evening, the house was dark as the flames died slowly in the hearth.

"Taeo?" she called softly from her position cuddled against his chest.

"Mmm?" His responding grunt was just as soft.

"Do you know why I started that conversation with you yesterday?"

"You mean that argument?"

She nudged his side with her elbow. "I was mad at myself. Guess I'm *still* mad at myself." Her lips twisted wryly. "I've watched you all these years—playing women so easily, breaking their hearts…. I swore I was smarter, *different.* I swore you'd never have that kind of power over me—to just snap your fingers and have me give up every bit of myself for just a shred of your time with my body."

Mataeo braced a muscular forearm behind her back, bringing her close and kissing the top of her head. "Is that such a bad thing?" He rubbed a lock of her hair between his fingers. "Spending my time with your body?"

The mere thought of it caused a lump of need to form in her throat.

"No. No, it's not. Not as long as we're here— protected and without the eyes and assumptions of the business world upon us." She grimaced at the idea and sought to calm herself by smoothing a hand across the chiseled breadth of his pecs. "A big part of me doesn't give a damn about what they think, but another part knows how much those assumptions could hurt us."

"Hey?" Mataeo curved his hand around her jaw. "Look at me. Do you understand that I don't expect us to pretend to be just business associates only to keep up appearances?"

"I know that."

Mataeo read her mind easily. "Is it a problem for you?"

Temple's smile showed pity. "You're so smart in so many things and in so many things you've got no clue at all." She pressed on his chest and pushed herself up to sit and stretch her fingers toward the dying fire. "How could it not be a problem for me when I've spent so long trying to get everybody to believe I haven't gotten where I am by being good on my back?"

Mataeo's striking features hardened noticeably and he pushed up to sit, as well. "What do you mean, 'trying to get everybody to believe'?"

"I'm not…perceived the same as you, Taeo." She smiled at the look he sent her way. "Men are always surprised by that, when it's *men* who keep those perceptions alive."

He had no comeback and patiently waited for her to continue.

"You get kudos for every woman you bring to your bed. I get called all sorts of sluts and gold diggers for every deal I help close. I get called a slut every time you buy me a new 'token of appreciation.'" She lifted her hands toward the living room's high ceiling.

In a sudden display of agility and strength, Mataeo caught both her arms and lifted her over to him. "Who said that to you?" He gave her a little jerk once she was straddling his lap.

Temple shook her head, not about to name names. She didn't see the point. "I'm not the only woman who goes through this kind of mess, but that doesn't mean I have to like or accept it." She shifted her gaze toward the windows and gave a nod.

"Looks like the sun's coming out in time to set. We better go." She pushed off Mataeo and went to collect her things.

Although it was Temple who got caught and drenched in the rainstorm, the rest of the Grahame women felt Mataeo was more deserving of being pampered.

When they arrived back at her mother's house, Temple learned that her sisters had a prime dinner planned. She and Mataeo took their places at the kitchen table and listened while Helena proudly shared the intended menu. Gladys set a steamy mug of coffee in front of Mataeo while Aliya announced that it was just the way he liked it.

When the lights flickered and then went out completely, Temple didn't even try to hide her laughter.

"Hope you enjoy that coffee," she told Mataeo once she'd teased her sisters relentlessly. "I doubt your caretakers know how to heat water without electricity."

"Now don't worry, baby." Aileen came by to pat Mataeo's shoulder once she'd sent the dismayed younger women off for candles and flashlights. "Temple and I can handle it from here."

"May I help?"

Aileen waved off Mataeo's offer. "You just enjoy your coffee, sugar."

It was almost impossible to see in the kitchen, but Temple and her mother worked by the light of the moon. Mataeo sipped his coffee and listened to the clattering of drawers opening and closing. The girls eventually returned with the flashlights and candles. Soon, the entire lower level of the house was aglow.

Mataeo saw what all the clattering was about. The ancient-looking woodstove in the corner was more than a showpiece.

"That thing works?" he asked.

Aileen and Temple laughed over Mataeo's surprise.

"You sound just like my girls the first time they had a full meal prepared on this," Aileen reminisced, but didn't veer far from her task of lighting kindling for the fire.

Mataeo leaned forward in his chair. "I always wondered how people cooked on those things."

Again, Aileen laughed. "Watch and learn, sugar. Watch and learn."

The group sat down to a candlelit dinner courtesy of the old school. Mataeo repeatedly remarked on how impressed he was and it was no exaggeration. Everything was cooked to perfection, flavorful and satisfying.

"How'd you learn to cook like this?" he asked Temple as the sound of mixed conversations and dinnerware hovered in the kitchen.

Temple merely nodded toward her mother.

Mataeo smirked and helped himself to another biscuit. "I should've asked why it appealed to you to *want* to learn to cook like this."

"Never know when those skills might come in handy," she sang while passing him the butter. "That's what we keep trying to tell those three." She spoke a bit louder for her younger sisters' benefit.

The girls simply waved off Temple's musings and

dinner continued in comfortable silence. Beef stir-fry
with rice pilaf and biscuits. Such a contemporary meal
prepared in such an old-fashioned way.

Mataeo didn't think he'd ever enjoyed a meal more.
He knew that was because of the woman seated next
to him. Contemporary yet old-fashioned—he'd never
met anyone like Temple and he highly doubted that he
ever would.

She appealed to him on so many levels and she
always had. Those earlier events had been of the non-
romantic variety, though. That had all changed now.

"Looks like all the lights are out, Mama." Aliya had
left the table to check past the windows and noticed that
the other houses spaced out along the shore were dark.
"Guess the neighbors are dining by candlelight, too."

"Storm's getting closer," Aileen noted.

"Gosh, I hope it doesn't ruin Greg and Tess's party,"
Helena mentioned, her small nose scrunching in dis-
gust.

"Well, it rained today and they weren't calling for
it until the end of the week." Gladys reached for the
bowl of rice pilaf. "Maybe we'll get it all out of the way
before the big night."

"Oh, baby, I hope this won't mess up your last look
at the other house." Aileen patted Temple's thigh.

"It's all right Mama." Temple offered her a quick
smile. "So long as I can get inside the house—it's the
one I really wanted to see again." She looked up and
caught Mataeo's stare. Hiding her smile, she returned
her attention to her dinner.

Chapter 15

Streams of bubbles oozed down the pearly porcelain siding of the deep square tub that was situated in the middle of the huge bathroom. Sloshing water mingled with the moans and soft suggestive conversation coming from the tub's two occupants.

Mataeo leaned his head against the padded rest and clutched Temple's hips tighter to direct her movements.

"Temp...dammit, wait...."

"Wait, why?" She exchanged her circular movements on his erection for up-and-down strokes that made him feel even harder beneath the thin sheet of the condom he wore.

Mataeo gave up trying to control her moves. He cupped one of the breasts that bounced before his face.

Temple melted when he took the tip into his mouth. "Mmm...I don't think Ken meant for us to check out the houses this way," she gasped, lashes feeling weighty as she savored the deep penetration of his sex inside hers.

"Having different experiences might help you decide." Mataeo winced as Temple's clutch and release on his shaft sent a piercing wave of pleasure through him.

"Taeo…" Temple let her head fall back as she focused on reaching her peak. She rode him without mercy.

"Hell…" His hand tightened at her hip but he knew better than to unsettle her. "Not ready yet, Temp…"

"Sorry." The apology was halfhearted and she took from him what she wanted.

Mataeo couldn't resist following suit. His arms came around her when he sat up a bit straighter. Powerful hands squeezed her slick shoulders, arms and back as his own climax took hold.

Gradually, the water left in the tub began to calm. Temple and Mataeo lay entwined in the fading bubbles while they came down off their high.

"Did you make a decision?" He squeezed her thigh, stroking it with a possessive hand.

"Not sure." She trailed her mouth across his collarbone. "The tub definitely puts it high on the list."

"It's a great tub." Mataeo forced his eyes open and observed the space. "I like the way it's sectioned off from the shower—in the middle of the room. I've had a thing for tubs since I was a kid."

Temple grazed her thumbnail about the male nipple protruding from the impressively sculpted pec. "I'm guessing there wasn't a great selection of them at the orphanage."

Mateo's chuckle rumbled throughout his big frame. "There wasn't a great selection of anything there."

Temple sobered somewhat. "As long as we've known each other…I don't know anything about that part of your life."

He gathered her closer. "Not much to say about it. But as bad as it was, I had rather been there instead of a foster home."

"And you never wanted to find your parents?" Temple pushed up more and studied his handsome face, still relaxed as he lounged in the tub.

"I was more interested in finding my salvation."

"Hence, North Shipping." She smiled when he shrugged. "Didn't you ever wonder about your name? Your real name?"

"I know it." His expression remained closed. "The day I finally had enough guts to run away, I changed it." He opened his eyes then to gauge her reaction. "I found my first name in a grocery store while I was lifting cans of soup for my dinner—packaging company on the back of a can…Mateo…sounded tough." He smirked.

Temple shook her head in wonder. "And your last name?"

"I flagged down a truck driver. He asked if I was goin' north. I turned down the ride—I was headed south…." He brushed a lock of her hair across his jaw. "I thought *North* sounded good, though…strong." He smirked again when Temple laughed at his reasoning.

"I lived by my wits—what wits I had." He shrugged. "Made it through college with a crapload of grad loans and workin' my ass off." He kissed her forehead.

"When you came into my life, it was like God had sent me my own personal angel. A reward for a job well done raising myself."

Temple frowned over the comparison. "Some angel. You helped *me* more than the other way around."

"Little did you know." Mataeo shifted in the tub to get a better look at her face. "I love you." He tightened his hold on her when she would have moved away.

"Mataeo—"

"I love you in every way a man could and should love a woman." His provocatively intense cocoa gaze slid down to her bare breasts glistening from the cool water. "I know you still think I'm full of it, but there's going to come a time when you'll just have to risk it. To say to hell with it and trust me." He brought his stare back to her face and studied her closely. "The one thing you should never do is to expect me to back off." He shook his head once. "You know me well enough to know I'd never do that." He dropped a hard kiss to her mouth and left her alone in the tub.

The next few days weren't exactly tense, but there was a certain distance between Mataeo and Temple. Thankfully, it wasn't recognized by the others. Everyone was toiling away, growing busier as the anniversary party moved closer.

Such was the case the morning of the party. Aileen and the girls had gone out to meet with the caterers and musicians. Despite the weather's unpredictability, the plans were still on to have an outdoor event.

The aroma of breakfast was already filling the

kitchen that morning. The party meal was slated to be a buffet affair.

Mataeo followed the fragrance of food down the back stairway. PDA in hand, he scanned his calendar for the next two weeks. He wasn't sure of Temple's schedule or how long she intended to remain in Charleston visiting with her family.

His appointments for the next two weeks could easily be reset, but was it necessary? The possibility was slim that she'd come back to Wilmington with him to resume the business portion of their lives. To her, that would be like telling everyone they'd been right about her from the jump.

Still, he knew his words were working past that suspicious veneer of hers. He couldn't be angry with her for wanting to take care of herself—to protect her heart. He couldn't tell whether she believed him when he said he wouldn't walk away. He only knew that for any of this to have a chance of working, they had to share the same turf. If that meant he had to stay on there until she took him at his word, then so be it.

Mataeo leaned against the wall along the stairway leading down to the kitchen. He was focused on making a few final entries to his calendar when he heard voices. Correction. He heard one voice—Temple's.

"I've already put everything in place. I have to see it through," Temple said to Megaleen as they spoke by phone.

"But, honey, is that necessary now with you and Mataeo coming to an understanding?"

"An understanding, Meg?" Temple fumbled with the frayed edge of the orange-and-white bandana she'd tied

around her head. "He doesn't need me there. With all
this between us, it'd just be one long mess, which is all
it's been since we got caught up in this." She puffed
out her cheeks and shook her head. "No, it's better for
me to just go on and resign like I've been planning to
do for the last year and a half. I think I've waited long
enough already."

Mataeo heard a tiny crunch and realized he held the
electronic planner so tightly that he was breaking its
casing. Rage funneled up inside him from somewhere
deep. Blindly, he turned and made his way back upstairs.

"Temp? You there?"

"Yeah—yeah, Meg, I—" Temple stopped talking
when she thought she heard something just outside the
kitchen.

"Honey, you know all this is just your fear talking."

"Yeah…" Temple turned back into the conversation and took a seat at the big round table. Silence held
the line while she considered (and agreed) with Meg's
words. "Yeah, I am scared. And with that in mind, how
could I ever make this work? All I would do is keep
second-guessing myself, drive Mataeo crazy until he'd
say to hell with all the drama."

Meg's rich laughter filled the line. "That's definitely
a possibility. But I think you owe it to him, hon. Hell,
you owe it to yourself—give him a chance. You've both
said how much you love each other, now prove it. You
can't make me believe you don't want to."

Temple groaned. "No, no, I can't even make myself
believe that. If only I could stop…"

"Putting yourself in other women's shoes?"

"Hmph. Something like that."

"You think you're the only woman who's ever done that? Had a fear of winding up an ex-lover, especially when the man she's interested in is known to be the hit-and-run type?"

"All right you've made your point." Temple leaned over to rest an elbow on her knee. "You're sayin' I'm gonna have to risk it."

"Risk it or spend your life wondering what might have been."

Again, silence lingered. Eventually, Meg's sigh came through the line.

"So I guess you've got enough to think on. We'll talk when you get back, okay?"

"Thanks, Meg." Temple clicked off her cell and then stared out at the scenery for a while.

Gradually, however, her suspicion returned. She left the table and strolled toward the back stairway. She eyed it thoughtfully.

The weather was exceedingly cooperative for the party, which began just before sunset. Other than a slight wind and the slightest nip in the air, the climate was wonderful. Couples held hands while strolling the gorgeous Grahame property with its beautiful starlit view of the horizon. Others enjoyed dancing right on the beach.

Temple saw Mataeo at the bar set up across from the dance area. She took a deep breath, gathering a bit more courage before she approached him.

"Ginger ale, please," she asked the bartender while

taking the chair next to Mataeo. "Mama and the girls did a good job, huh?" she asked.

"Yeah. Damn good." The response was clipped, hard.

"Thanks." Temple accepted the drink from the woman behind the bar. "Looks like the storm held up, after all."

"So we're gonna talk about the weather?"

Temple took his obvious mood to be work related. Concerned, she gathered a fistful of her casually elegant tunic dress with its extra-long sleeves and scooted closer to him on her chair.

"Is everything okay back at the office?" she asked and watched him clench a fist.

"Tell me just how this works, Temp. When we talk business am I supposed to forget how it feels when I'm inside you? Hmm?"

Temple bit her lip and decided it was better to beg off from the discussion. "I only came to ask you to dance, Mataeo," she quietly explained while sliding down off the seat.

"Well then, by all means." Mataeo drained his glass and then almost dragged her to the dance floor.

"What the hell is wrong with you?" She shoved a hand against the crisp collarless dark olive shirt he wore outside black trousers.

Phony innocence clouded his very attractive face. "What could be wrong with me besides having to overhear the person I trust most discussing her plans to resign—plans she's had for a damn year and a half?"

She blinked in the face of his snarl. "You *did* overhear me."

He nodded and shifted his glare out over the crowd. "I heard enough."

Temple had a feeling that wasn't true. One look at him said this wasn't the time to discuss it further. She made a move to extract herself from his embrace. Mataeo simply squeezed her closer and she trembled at the feel of his well-made body fusing against hers.

"Taeo, have you thought that maybe it *is* better for me to go? I mean, we could probably use the space and time to—to think if we're really ready for this."

He took her by the chin in a none-too-gentle hold. "You'll go when I'm ready for you to leave. For now, I'd settle for seeing you back in Wilmington on Monday morning bright and early for breakfast at the Cape. And bring your attorney," he advised before brushing past her.

Chapter 16

Monday morning, the Cape was teeming with the usual high-traffic crowd stopping by to enjoy a good Southern breakfast before heading off to the various endeavors of the day. Meg and Temple were among the crowd, thanking their waiter for the coffees he set on the table.

"Did they say what this was about?" Temple asked once the polite college-aged kid had walked off.

Megaleen added cream to her coffee while shaking her head. "Not really. Cora just got a call and was told to be sure I was there." She blew across the surface of the coffee. "I thought maybe *you'd* have a better idea than me."

"No more than what I told you before." Temple reached for a spoon but made no attempt to use it.

"So he overheard our conversation and you didn't bother to tell him he only heard half of it."

Temple winced. "I got it, Meg, all right? Trust me, I've beat myself up enough over this."

Meg was about to sip her coffee and then changed her mind. "Well then." She stared across the packed dining room. "Guess we're about to find out the consequences of your choice."

Temple followed Megaleen's gaze and saw Mataeo heading across the dining room…with his attorney.

"Why's Eaton Broward here?" Temple's voice was a whisper. She risked a glance toward Meg, who appeared as clueless as she.

"Morning, ladies!" Eaton Broward was a tall, well-built man in his early fifties. He had an easy manner that won him tons of friends outside the courtroom. Inside the courtroom was another matter. The man took no prisoners.

"How you doin', Meg?" Mataeo greeted her with a warm handshake and kiss on the cheek while Eaton greeted Temple in much the same manner.

"Just fine, Mataeo." Meg couldn't keep the hushed, intrigued tone from her voice. She was no more immune to the man's intense sex appeal and subtle charm than any other woman.

Mataeo decided not to waste his charm on Temple just then. "Morning," was the extent of his greeting to her as he claimed a seat next to Meg at the round table.

"Eaton, what's this about?" Temple asked, having coolly ignored her boss's chilly acknowledgment.

"Well, Temple, Mataeo just informed me of your decision to leave North Shipping. I can't tell you how sorry we all are to hear that. You and my client have made a great team over the years."

Despite Eaton's matter-of-fact tone, Temple was stunned. She turned a wide gaze toward Mataeo, whose expression gave away nothing.

"There're just a few papers needing your signature." Eaton was going through the beige portfolio that complimented the brown three-piece he wore to the meeting.

Business at the table was interrupted when the waiter returned for the gentlemen's drink orders. Temple kept her eyes on Mataeo the whole time, only tuning back in when Eaton addressed her again in his hearty voice.

"Now, there's the mandatory six-month period before you can leave. If you recall, this time frame allows us to get all the paperwork thoroughly completed and it also gives you time to put folks in place to handle your workload and get them up to speed."

"Well, you know how efficient Temple is, Eaton." Mataeo chose to speak, tugging on the cuff of his silver-gray suit coat as he did so. "She's already got folks in place to handle what it is she does for me." Suggestion lurked in his deep-set and appealing stare.

Temple was beyond livid. Wrapping her hands around her coffee mug, she envisioned herself dashing its steamy contents into Mataeo's face. Instead, she reached for Megaleen's hand beneath the table and squeezed.

"Now, now, there's no rush." Eaton had tuned in to the thick tension in his midst. "We do have six months, after all."

Meg coughed to hide her moan of pain. Temple was almost crushing her hand.

Eaton reached into the beige portfolio again. "There

is one document that we'll need your signature on ASAP." He cleared his throat while opening the folder that he turned toward Temple.

Releasing Meg's hand, Temple leaned over to scan the document. She looked up at Eaton with a questioning glare.

"It's a statement of confidentiality, Temple," he clarified.

The question in her hazel eyes turned to disbelief when she looked at Mataeo. Without argument and without looking away from him, she scrawled her name across the page and tossed the pen.

Eaton caught it before it skipped over the edge. "Thank you, Temple. This is all the business we had. I do hope we won't be strangers once you've moved on to greener pastures." Silence followed and then Eaton raised his heavy brows toward his client. "Anything else?"

Smiling then, Mataeo stood and buttoned his jacket. "I guess that's it for now. We've got six months to get everything else in place, right?" He waved a hand over the table. "You two eat up now. It's on me."

The waiter returned for orders after Mataeo and Eaton had gone.

Meg flexed her aching hand and gave the young man a tight smile. "Could I have a bucket of ice, please?"

The flaring, uneven hem of Temple's black skirt rippled just below her knee and emphasized her shapely legs as she stormed down the executive hall. She bolted through Mataeo's open office door and slammed it shut behind her.

"I wanted that to stay open." He barely looked up from the papers he studied while leaning against the front of his desk.

Temple shoved her hands against his back. "How could you humiliate me like that?"

"Humiliate?" Mataeo stroked his jaw and sat on the edge of the desk. "I thought Eaton was very professional."

"How could you ask me to sign a confidentiality agreement?"

He shrugged, watching his hands as he rubbed them one over the other. "You keep so much from me these days, how am I to know where your loyalties lie?"

Temple could have screamed. She focused on her foot tapping heatedly against the carpet and worked to raise her level of calm.

"Why would you want to keep me around for six months if you can't trust me?"

"Call it payback." His eyes were still on his hands.

Temple nodded as though the confession was of no real surprise. "Well, you can think again if you expect me to stick around here for another six months and go through hell with you."

He slammed a fist on the edge of the desk before pushing up from it. "That shouldn't be too hard for you, should it?" He stalked her then. "According to you, our time together's been one long mess."

She closed her eyes on the memory of the conversation he had half heard. She was opening her mouth to tell him that when he issued his challenge.

"Unless you prefer to be sued?"

Eyes narrowed, Temple leaned back on her pumps. "You wouldn't."

"Wouldn't I?"

"And if I countersued?"

He laughed. "On what grounds?"

Temple spread her hands. "I think I could make a case for harassment."

The laughter ceased and the smile turned menacing. "Surely not sexual?" He moved closer. "Not after all the remarkable things you've done to me over the last week and a half."

She slapped him.

Mateo responded with a punishing kiss to her mouth. The "punishment," however, was fleeting and grew lusty as it coaxed a response.

The fight left Temple as she surrendered to the need he teased out of her. She was moaning and bathing his tongue with hers when he smoothly stepped back from their kiss.

"Is that what this is, Mateo?" she asked after taking a moment to catch her breath. "Your need to win at all costs? Or is it just about the satisfaction you get from acting like a child?" She swallowed with great effort when he moved closer again and trailed his nose across her jaw before his mouth settled against her ear.

"No, Temp. This is about being pissed as hell."

Temple went back to her office with her mind set on packing and leaving. To hell with Mateo North and his documents and decrees. Papers and files flew all over the desk, some settling to the floor. She realized she was only making a mess and took a moment to catch her breath. She was leaning against the corner of the desk, staring out at her view when a knock hit the office door.

"Temple Grahame?" the young Asian woman inquired.

"Yes." She managed a smile and went to meet the bike messenger in the middle of the room.

Temple signed for the thin envelope and then returned to perch on the edge of her desk again. Inside the package, she found an invite to a celebration affair from Manson Yates.

The invitation was bittersweet. Temple thought of the many deals she and Mataeo had worked on. All that success, and to have it all come down to *this.* She scanned the invite—*this* was the last.

Another knock fell on the door. Ike Melvin stuck his head into the room. "Temple G!"

The bright greeting brought a smile to her face and she felt happier to leave her desk that time. They met in the center of the room for hugs.

"I've missed you, girl." He squeezed her tight.

"Went to see my mom in Charleston."

"Everything okay down there?" He studied her with honest concern and smiled when she nodded. "Well, everybody's floating on a cloud with this Yates thing in the bag. Excitement to the highest power in my neck of the woods." He shook his head and regarded her as if in awe. "Gotta give all the credit to you."

"Mmm. Please don't." Temple puffed out her cheeks and moved away from Ike.

"Don't be modest, Temp. If it wasn't for all your

work on the survey expedition, we'd have never impressed Yates the way we did."

"You're sweet." She reached out and cupped his cheek for a brief moment. "But a lot of players had a role in us securing this deal."

"That may be." Ike followed when Temple headed back toward her desk. "But not according to the boss. You were all Mataeo could talk about when we had the lunch with Yates."

"Is that right?" She folded her arms over the coral-colored blouse she wore.

"Yeah, that's right. We all had a round of drinks after lunch. If your ears weren't burnin' they should've been. Like I said, you were all the man could talk about."

Temple tried to consider it and then shook her head as if the possibility were too much to comprehend. *How quickly things changed,* she thought. From accolades and compliments to confidentiality agreements and humiliation. Before her anger could fully resurface, Ike was clearing his throat.

"Speaking of drinks." Some of the easiness left his handsome face. "I should apologize for what happened the night of the tour."

"Apologize? Ike, what?"

"Don't tell me you forgot the way I acted like a drunken buffoon?"

She laughed, remembering then. "It's okay."

"No. No, it wasn't."

"You were just excited over the event and how well everything was going."

"Well…I appreciate you making excuses for me but I know I acted like a jerk."

"So can we just forget it?" Temple bartered with an outstretched hand, smiling when he accepted the shake.

Ike looked as though he wanted to say more. Instead, he pushed one hand into his pinstriped trouser pocket and nodded at the invite she was still holding.

"You gonna make an appearance?"

Temple scrunched her nose and turned the envelope over in her hands. "Guess I better since I *am* the reason we got the deal." She sent Ike a teasing wink and they shared laughter.

"So, um…would you care for going together?" His manner held a smidgen of awkwardness.

Again, Temple studied the invite.

"I promise only one drink the entire night."

Temple couldn't help but smile. Still, her mind was set on Mataeo and what he'd think of her going to the party with Ike. Then her thoughts shifted to the dreaded confidentiality statement and the embarrassment she'd endured that morning.

She nodded and Ike's expectant look turned into satisfaction.

"I'd love to, Ike. As long as you don't expect me to stay the entire night. Schmoozing at parties has never been my thing."

Ike's laughter returned. "It's a deal!"

After Ike's departure, Temple set aside the invitation and tried to put another dent in her packing. Her cell phone began to vibrate beneath a few folders. She answered before voice mail could take over. It was Kendall.

"Hey—sorry," Temple told him in the same breath.

"I shouldn't have skipped town without making that decision like I promised."

"Temple, it's fine. Everything's been cleared up and you've got nothing to worry about."

"Ken?" Temple switched the phone to her other ear. "What do you mean everything's been cleared up? Did you sell the places?"

"No, Temp, nothin' like that. You can take your time making a decision on them is all."

"Well—"

"Hey, hey, don't go lookin' a gift horse in the mouth, all right?"

It was all just a little too neat for Temple. "Ken, do you realize how this sounds? You had other people interested, remember?"

"And they say they're not in any rush so long as they get first dibs on the remaining props once you make your decision."

"Ken—"

"Look, Temp, I hate to do this but I need to go. Talk to you soon, all right?"

Temple was poised to ask another question when the connection dissolved. She was staring dumbfounded at the phone when the third knock of the afternoon sounded on the door.

She turned to greet the visitor with a smile that faded when she saw that it was Mataeo standing just inside the room. She tensed immediately while observing his characteristically cool stance.

"Coming to check on me, then? Making sure I'm not stealing office supplies?"

His smile collided with a wince. "Guess I deserve that."

"Hmph." She rolled her eyes. "You deserve a lot more than that."

"I came to apologize, Temp."

Temple practically tripped over her wedge-heeled pumps when she turned to face him. "What's going on?" Her light eyes narrowed in suspicion.

"I just want to apologize." He moved farther into the office.

"And what about being pissed as hell?"

"Temple." His voice was soft as he scratched the corner of a sleek brow. "Can you blame me? Don't answer that." He raised a hand when she appeared eager to do so. "Temple, my being pissed off was about *us*— not the business. I never should have mixed the two. I humiliated you for no reason."

Temple had no words then. Mataeo North never apologized. At least, she'd never heard him doing it. Quite frankly, she had no words because she was simply too stunned to speak.

He shortened what distance was left between them. Bowing his head, he took both her hands in his and squeezed them. He brought them to his mouth and brushed his lips across her knuckles.

Temple commanded every part of her body to remain unresponsive.

"I went and did the one thing I swore I wouldn't. I hurt you. I hope you can forgive me for that." He took a deep breath and met her gaze.

"You're free to go anytime you want—which I'm pretty sure you would do, anyway." His smile was weak. "After Eaton cursed me out for acting like a fool this morning, we drew up another document to override that stupid codicil in your contract. Who the hell suggested we put that in there in the first place?" he muttered.

Temple smiled.

Mataeo's striking features had sharpened. He cupped Temple's cheek, shaking his head as if he were in awe of her. Then he kissed her cheek and left.

Mataeo and Temple met that afternoon for a meeting with the new team organized to oversee Temple's vast duties. The team consisted of Winnie Osmond, Edmund Jansen, Erica Staling, David Cafrey and Barry Heckel.

Temple had been on pins and needles for much of the day. She was so preoccupied thinking about what mood she'd find Mataeo in. She prayed he wouldn't scare the group too badly to want to work closely with him.

She needn't have worried. Mataeo seemed to be in great spirits. He kept the group of younger recruits laughing and relaxed enough to inquire about their various job duties. The meeting culminated with the setting of future gatherings before Temple resigned her post.

"Thanks for being so great just now." Temple had lagged behind after the crowd dispersed.

Mataeo loosened his tie and shrugged out of the suit coat. "They're a good group. You chose well."

"Thanks." Her eyes lingered on the breadth of his back beneath the crisp shirt and vest he was in the process of unbuttoning. "I, um…I appreciate you taking the time," she added, somewhat somberly.

"Not a problem." Mataeo nodded while closing and setting the lock to the three entrances to his office.

Temple rubbed her hands along the sleeves of her blouse. "Everything's gotten so crazy." She cleared her throat and shook her head over all that had happened. "So tense," she added.

Mataeo grimaced, dropping his tie and suit coat to a chair. "Amen to the 'tense' part."

"Well…" she breathed, facing him with a feigned resigned look in place. "It'll be better once I'm out of here."

"Will it?" He crossed the room.

"It needs to be this way, Taeo." She swallowed yet maintained her footing as he crowded her.

"Who says it has to be this way?" He finished unbuttoning the black pinstriped vest and cupped her elbow while guiding her back. "Who made that rule, Temp? All these folks you're tryin' to put on a charade for?"

"I'm not." Again she swallowed when his nose outlined the curve of her jaw. "I'm not putting on a charade."

Mataeo had been steadily easing her back until she was flush against the bookcases that lined an entire wall. "Then I guess that means you won't mind this, hmm?"

Temple had barely a second to breathe his name before his tongue was in her mouth and enticing hers to play nice. She didn't disappoint him. She couldn't.

"Is this one for the road?" She was breathless, unable to resist the dig when he broke the kiss to lavish more below her ear.

He chuckled, just barely. "It's whatever you want it to be."

He was kissing her again, applying far more pressure than previously. The hands cupping Temple's elbows had curved about her hips, and then lower to cradle her bottom.

Temple drove her tongue against his hungrily in response to him pressing her into his impressive sex. Tiny whimpers lifted from her throat whenever he released her mouth to change the angle of his kiss. She took in the fabulous scent of the cologne clinging to his skin and shuddered at the arousal staking her every time she inhaled.

Mataeo squeezed her, drawing her impossibly closer. Then, he let one hand venture the healthy expanse of her thigh before tugging it higher near his hip. His free hand plundered beneath the hem of her skirt, searching for the edge of her panties.

Temple's cry was muffled beneath the onslaught of another kiss when his fingers vanished inside the crotch and caressed her drenched core. Her hands weakened where they spanned his shoulders, all her focus was on the pleasure he gave.

Mataeo tugged the lacy white lingerie at her hips until the panties tumbled around the pumps on her feet. Temple pushed the vest from his back while stepping from the material tangled at her heels. She unbuttoned his shirt, peeling it from his back but leaving it to dangle from the material still tucked into his trousers.

A deeper moan claimed Temple and she let her forehead rest on his chest when he released her mouth. She was on the verge of a delicious climax and unconsciously pleaded with him not to stop. She turned her face into his neck, squeezing her eyes closed when he added a third finger to the fondling.

"No, please," she begged when he withdrew mid-stroke.

Mataeo was unmindful of her fists beating his back as he lifted her effortlessly, carrying her behind his desk. Settling on the monstrous leather chair, he straddled her across his lap.

Temple ceased the blows she rained down on him once she observed her new position. Biting down on her lip, she watched Mataeo relieving her of her skirt, blouse and bra.

Ravenously, he suckled one nipple while brushing the other beneath his thumb. His hand at the small of her back kept her right where he wanted her.

Curving her hands over the arms of the chair, Temple rotated herself against Mataeo. She arched her back, pushing more breast into his mouth and shivering in delight when he greedily accepted.

Mataeo muttered an obscenity and dropped a hand to one of the desk drawers. Rummaging around inside for a second or three, he extracted a condom package, which he pressed into Temple's palm.

Temple could scarcely free him from the confines of his dark trousers she was so enthralled with the feel of him nibbling and suckling the tips of her breasts. Mataeo eased her back after some time, only maintaining the thumb brushes to her nipple as he undid his belt and trouser fastening.

Temple watched as though awed by the erection straining the zipper, which he left in place for her to handle. She managed it, feeling her heart pounding in her ears when his honey-colored sex was bared to her gaze. She drew her hand along the wide, rigid length of his shaft.

"Temple, please..."

The request was her undoing and she showed mercy. Some. Applying the condom proved to be sensuously torturing as Temple rolled down the latex with maddening slowness.

The second their protection was in place, Mataeo caught her hips and settled her intimately. He kept her fused atop him, refusing any movement and just savoring....

Temple wouldn't let herself acknowledge the fact that this was the last time she'd experience ecstasy. The last time she'd be pleasured by the man she adored. She melted on him, open to whatever he wanted, taking whatever he wanted to give.

Again he cupped her bottom, moving her to the pace he set. His head fell back on the chair and he squeezed his eyes shut amidst the satisfaction she provided as she gloved him. Temple's breathing came in short, hiccupping gasps. Her hands splayed weakly across his massive chest, too affected by him hard and throbbing inside her to do anything more than let him bend her to his desire.

Mataeo took as much as he gave. He was working to stifle his own voices, as well. They were voices that would have stirred his anger over the fact that he was about to lose her. He was about to lose her when he had finally, truly found her.

Chapter 17

The proprietors of the Wagner Hotel were used to handling elaborate requests for their patrons. The establishment was where Wilmington's elite met to do everything from enjoying some of the best pasta and seafood the East Coast had to offer, to celebrating the close of some of the biggest deals its upscale diners put together.

That evening, the Yates organization had the place closed down for a private party to celebrate the turnover of Manson Yates's highly regarded group of clients to North Shipping. Guests enjoyed the best in Scotch, bourbon and other liquors in addition to fragrant wines and delicious appetizers. Dinner was to be served once everyone on the entire one-hundred-and-seventy-five-person guest list had arrived. No one complained, the conversations were as delightful as the appetizers, the environment and the incomparable view of the city skyline.

"Guess I should've rented a tux," Ike said to Temple when they arrived at the shimmering ballroom.

She laughed, scanning the room of formal dressers. She did take note of a few who were dressed quite casually and she pointed them out to her date. Her easy manner and soft chuckling stopped midstream when she saw Mataeo across the dining room.

It was difficult to tell whether he'd come alone or with one of the four women that were surrounding him and laughing wildly at whatever he'd just said.

Temple cleared her throat while working to clear her face of emotion.

"Look, I'm gonna go grab a drink to nurse," Ike said, the look on his face proving that he'd seen the emotion she'd been trying to hide. He leaned close to prop her chin up with his index finger.

"Why don't you go and rescue your man from that mob?"

Her eyes widened. Lips parted but no sound emerged.

Ike grinned. "Don't try hiding it. You can't."

"Can't what?" she whispered around her heart in her throat.

"Hell, Temple, anybody with eyes can see you're in love with the guy."

She hid her face in her hands and groaned.

Ike rubbed her shoulder. "You've done a good job of hiding it until lately. I'm pretty sure Mataeo's clued into it, but I'll bet he didn't have a clue before."

The revelations were doing little to settle her stomach. She pressed a hand on the side gathers on the chic ankle-length dress she wore. The midnight-blue material accentuated the flawless coffee tone of her skin. Her hair flew loose and bounced about her shoulders. Dangling silver earrings brushed the neckline of the dress as they shimmered.

"Sorry, Temp." Ike squeezed her arm reassuringly. "I didn't see it until I had the chance to work around y'all myself. Both of you were pretty much dead giveaways then."

Temple watched him in confusion. "Why'd you ask me to come with you tonight?"

Ike shrugged, appearing sheepish as he shoved his hands into the pockets of his suit.

"Every man wonders what it's like to live in Mataeo North's world." He studied Mataeo with the women across the room and then looked at Temple. "What a lot of us wonder about most is what it feels like to have you on his arm." He shrugged. "The guy's a lucky dog." He kissed her cheek. "I'll catch up with you later."

Temple watched Ike until he'd disappeared into the massive crowd. She was jumping a few moments later when Megaleen poked her in the back.

"Walk with me." Meg didn't wait for acceptance. She took Temple's arm and led her down from the entryway steps.

"You're hoggin' all the attention standin' up here at the front of the room."

"Mataeo apologized for the other morning," Temple shared as they weaved through the crowd.

"Yeah, and even had that codicil overwritten." Meg paused to grab two champagne flutes from a passing server. "So are you still doubting how he feels about you?" As Ike had done earlier, Meg kissed her friend's cheek. "And for heaven's sake, how long are you gonna pretend he's not here? Wonderful event, Mr. Yates," she said before sauntering off.

Temple turned with a refreshing smile in place for Manson Yates. "Thank you for the party Mr.— Manson." She laughed when he gazed at her sternly for attempting to address him formally.

"It's me who should be thanking you." Manson squeezed her forearm, bared by the quarter-length cut of the dress sleeves. "Without all that impressive work it may've taken me a lot longer to decide that North was the right fit for my clients."

"You sound like you knew all along that you'd go with Mataeo."

Manson took a swallow of his bourbon. "I pretty much knew it the day I met the kid. He's got that same scrappy, hungry look I had back when I was just startin' out."

Temple laid her hand on the man's shoulder as she laughed. "I don't think Mataeo's been hungry in a long time."

"Well, it's true that he's earned a lot of success, but the kid's definitely still hungry."

Temple angled her head. "How can you tell?"

Manson Yates barely raised his shoulder when he shrugged. "I can tell by the way he looks at you. North! Get this lady on the dance floor before someone beats you to it."

Before Temple could turn, she felt herself being pulled back against a granite wall of flesh. She would have known it was Mataeo behind her without Yates's greeting.

"I was just about to do that, sir," Mataeo rumbled. He squeezed Temple's upper arms and pressed his mouth next to her ear.

"Join me?" he asked.

She could only nod.

The Wagner's music of choice was old-school R & B, which may have seemed out of place among what appeared to be a rather conservative crowd. But the guests seemed to have no complaints about the grooves they swayed to.

Mataeo pulled Temple against him and they enjoyed the last few bars of Eugene Wilde's "Gotta Get You Home Tonight."

When the song faded into Earth, Wind and Fire's "Love's Holiday" Mataeo tightened his hold on Temple's waist and almost stopped swaying to the music altogether.

"I see you made Ike's night." He nodded and smiled across Temple's shoulder. "You finally went out with him."

"We only decided at the last minute." She mimicked his smile. "I see you decided on lots of company tonight." She referred to his four companions.

"I came here alone, Temp." His smile grew less smug. "They found me near the appetizers...." He trailed off, his nose grazing the side of her face while he massaged her back.

"Mataeo..."

"I don't care what anyone thinks about us." He

pulled back to stare at her with challenge in his deep-set browns.

Temple realized that most eyes were indeed on them. Mataeo curved his hand around her neck and gave the slightest tug.

"Maybe I don't care because I never had to." His gaze shifted for just a split second. "Guess right about now that's playing in my favor. I love you, Temple, and that's something I'll never doubt. When you're done caring what these people think about what does or doesn't go on between us, when you're ready to believe me when I tell you you're it for me—then you come and find me."

The hand on her neck flexed gently, holding Temple in place for the thorough kiss he planted.

Temple needed no coaxing, she was an instant participant. Without hesitation, she curled her fingers around the open collar of the black shirt he wore beneath a salt-and-pepper jacket. Tiny moans drifted from her throat while she took her time caressing his tongue with hers.

Mataeo added more force to the sultry kiss. He rotated his tongue over and under hers before suckling it with blatant possessiveness. He paused to kiss the corner of her mouth and then started the kiss all over again.

"Please, Taeo...plea—" she begged him not to go on and not to stop but to simply show mercy. Her legs felt like rubber. Every part of her throbbed. She knew if he asked, she would give him everything right there.

He brought the kiss to an end with one last peck on the corner of her mouth.

"Come to me," he spoke the words against her lips and then walked away from her.

A thunderstorm had taken shape as the evening progressed. It hadn't produced rain yet, only freakishly sharp lightning. Temple shuddered behind the wheel of her car each time a streak of it lanced across the sky.

In spite of the storm's eeriness, Temple couldn't stop thinking of the day back home in that downpour. She thought of how drenched she'd been and how Mataeo had…warmed her.

She blinked, shaking the erotic images from her mind. Best not to dwell on them, lest she find herself going over the side of the narrow road that led to Mataeo's house along the shore. She didn't even know if he was there. Since her trip to the office and the place he kept in town proved useless, this was her final option. Mataeo's command for her to come to him, while seductive, was quite vague.

Temple rested her head on the steering wheel, relieved by the sight of his silver SUV parked at a slant in the front yard.

God, let him be here. She realized she had no idea what he'd driven to the party. She left her car parked near the SUV and braced herself against the fierce wind while she headed toward the front steps. She knocked twice before remembering that she had a key.

"Taeo?" Her voice harbored caution as did the manner in which she ventured down the black corridor.

Temple felt her way along the wall, hoping to find a light switch. Her search was for nothing. The switch she found sparked no light. The freakish lightning had claimed the electricity as its victim.

"Mataeo?" Temple rubbed her hands across suddenly chilled arms. "Mataeo?" She made her way to the living room but stopped halfway to the wide balcony doors. There, she debated and decided she'd reached another dead end. When she turned to leave, she slammed right into him.

Her shriek filled the room as she braced her fists against his chest and bowed her head to catch her breath.

"You could've at least given me a hint about where you were going. I've been everywhere looking for you."

"Well, I guess that means you really wanted to find me then." The depth of his voice rivaled the thunder rumbling in the distance.

Apology fueled Temple's smile but she knew he couldn't see it in the dark. Words were required.

"I love you, Mataeo. I've loved you for so long. I've been *in love* with you for so long."

He took her by the arm. "More than you care about what everybody else thinks? More than you care about my track record with other women?"

"Yes. Yes, Mataeo."

His hold tightened on her arm suddenly and he tugged her to the balcony where the moonlight streamed in to offer a bit more illumination.

"I love you, Mataeo." Temple knew he needed to see her face when she said it. "I'm in love with you." She smoothed her hand across his flawless cheek. "And, yes, I love you more than I care about what anyone else thinks or your sordid history with your admirers." She smiled. "None of it matters, Taeo. I want the risk—" she stepped closer "—if you still want me."

Mataeo looked toward the balcony for a brief moment as he smiled over her question. Then, taking both her arms, he pulled her flush against him.

"You're all I want," he growled into her neck.

Contentment made her shudder. "I love you."

"I love you." His voice was still muffled into her skin.

Temple grazed his jaw with her nails and urged his head up. She initiated a kiss that sent Mataeo rearing back as he experienced an unexpected loss of strength in his legs.

Picking up where they left off at the party, the two began to move to a slow groove meant especially for them. They danced to the music of the thunder and the dazzle of the lightning.

Temple had no intention or desire to break their kiss until she felt her hand grow heavy beneath the weight of the gem he eased onto her finger.

"Mataeo—"

"I'm done with wasting time." He cradled her face in his hands. "Marry me."

Chapter 18

"Marry me." Mataeo smiled brightly at the sound of his fiancée's laughter.

"Yes, yes, yes and yes again. I think that brings the count to over a dozen times that you've asked me." Temple circled her arms around his waist and drew her hands up across his broad back.

Mataeo snuggled his face into the hollow of her shoulder. They cuddled after making love in the still unfurnished living room of the beach house at Edisto. Temple had finally made her choice and on so many levels.

"I'll ask and keep asking until you're all mine." He dropped kisses along the base of her neck.

She stretched lazily beneath him. "And just when will that be?"

Mataeo rolled to his back and took Temple across his chest. "Guess that's up to Miss Aileen, and once she decides which place'll be for the engagement party and which for the reception. We'll save the other for the honeymoon."

Temple smiled though the look in her eyes was curious. "What are you talking about?"

He squeezed her bottom and sighed dramatically. "Well, hell, Temp, these places were too great to risk losing and since you were takin' so long to make up your mind...I called Ken and told him we'd take 'em all."

"I knew it!" She slapped his shoulder. "I knew you were acting weird the last time we talked about this. You've never been able to lie worth a damn."

"So are you very mad that I, um...took over?"

"I'm not *very* mad." She couldn't stop her smile.

"Well, if you're itching to put an offer on the table, I'd be happy to sell you one."

"Oh, really?" She snuggled more intimately against him. "And at what price?"

Mataeo held her cheek. "A lifetime together."

Temple dropped a kiss into his palm. "Mmm...now, Mr. North, that's an offer I'd be very happy to accept."

Kisses took the place of all conversation then.

Mataeo and Temple left all wedding plans to Aileen Grahame. The woman wasted no time setting things in motion. She felt that the couple had waited long enough, after all. With the help of an aggressive team of assistants—her daughters—every detail was put in place for an understated yet exquisite event.

Reverend Reginald Gale presided over the nuptials exchanged along the beautiful stretch of beach that ran past the Grahameses' home. The vows were simple yet filled with meaning. It went without saying that a fair number of the guests were stunned to hear such heart-felt words of love, desire and devotion being spoken by Mataeo North. No one could deny that his commitment to the coffee-brown beauty at his side was anything but genuine.

"Well…I love what you haven't done with the place."

"Funny…" Mataeo told his wife when they entered the beach house from the back porch.

Temple strolled to the middle of the unfurnished kitchen and gave a minitwirl. "So Mama selected this one for the honeymoon, I guess?"

Mataeo tossed his keys to the counter. "Nah, she told me to take you someplace far away and not let you out of bed until we'd conceived her first grandchild."

Laughter filled the kitchen for several moments.

"I told her it was a deal but that I wanted to bring you here first."

Temple wrapped her arms around her waist and studied the glorious late-evening view of the Atlantic beyond the windows. "Things got pretty tense the first time we were here." She recalled their conversation before the fire where they warmed from the drenching rainstorm.

"Yeah." Mataeo walked over to draw her hands into his. "But I think it was the first time we started being really honest. I've thought a lot about that day."

"I see." She nestled close to him. "So you want to re-create it, is that it?"

"Well, there was one thing I'd have changed."

"Really?" Her hazel stare followed the path her thumb traced across the sultry curve of his mouth. She anticipated his kiss.

Instead, Mataeo broke the embrace and tugged her from the kitchen.

"What?" Temple stifled her question once she'd been pulled into the living room and saw that it had been transformed. "Taeo…"

"That damn floor was hard as hell," he explained, grinning at the way she studied the king sleigh bed turned down before the raging fire and flickering candlelight. "Did I do okay?" he asked when she looked at him.

Temple shrugged. "So far so good."

Sleek brows rising, Mataeo accepted the sly challenge. Pushing off the doorjamb he leaned against while watching her, he had her in his arms a moment later. One hand slipped inside the keyhole neckline of the figure-flattering cobalt-blue dress she wore. Expertly, and never taking his eyes off hers, he unfastened the front clasp of her bra.

Temple couldn't resist letting her lashes flutter when his middle finger began a slow caress of the valley between her breasts. Eagerly, she stood on her toes and instigated a hungry kiss.

Mataeo tangled his fingers in her healthy coarse locks and kept her close while drinking her in greedily. He backed her toward the bed, giving her a nudge that landed her in its center.

As he stood above watching her, Temple raised the hem of her dress. His seductive stare devoured every inch of skin she exposed to his view.

"Temple," he groaned when she wriggled out of the frock and was clothed only in a wispy pair of black lace panties.

Temple chewed her index nail and fixed him with a wicked glare. Her other arm resting above her head raised her full breasts to a more prominent level.

Mataeo looked as if he'd been presented with an unexpected treat. He wasn't about to let it go to waste. Kneeling to the bed, he hooked powerful hands around her upper thighs and pulled her closer. His nose outlined her belly button and the waistband of her panties. Temple began to nudge him suggestively, eventually pushing his head to the crotch of her underwear. She gasped loudly when his tongue caressed her through the fabric. Both hands lay above her head and she was helpless to do anything but thrust against his mouth. Expertly, he worked the panties from her hips and over her bottom.

The lacy garment clung to Temple's ankle when Mataeo raised her leg to give him more room to explore. Temple's thrusts gained more momentum when she felt his tongue bathing her sex before delving deep inside.

A low sound, barely audible, settled in his throat. He pulled her even closer to feast and withdrew when he felt her walls clench in a telltale fashion. It was Temple's turn to watch while he came out of his clothes.

Mataeo only went as far as freeing himself from the navy slacks he wore. Temple arched up, nibbling his jaw while guiding him inside her. Mataeo lost strength in every other part of his body. He braced his hands on either side of her head and gave himself over to her.

Temple clutched his butt, uttering a wavering moan when he was buried inside her. When Mataeo would have melted, she pushed him on his back and rolled her hips over him. She changed directions and laughed smugly when his gasp filled the room.

Mataeo took her hips, intending to take control and guide her movements. He winced when a sharper pang of sensation thrummed through him. His hands fell to the bed and then he brought them to his face and submitted.

Temple cupped her breasts while increasing the speed of her rotations. She shuddered and climaxed when he grew stiffer inside her. Mataeo's cocoa stare was narrowed, his own release at hand as he watched her.

For hours, the candlelit room was brought to life by the sounds of their passion.

A week later, the Norths were arriving at the house Mataeo kept in Wilmington at the shore.

"Change anything you want," he said, scanning the room with fleeting indifference before he followed Temple as she strolled the cool elegance of the living room.

"No, it's fine." She shook her head and laughed. "Hell, it's gorgeous. I've always thought so." She leaned against one of the three gray leather sofas the room boasted.

Mataeo didn't appear convinced as he leaned opposite her against the sofa. "It's your house, too, you know? You can do anything you like. Whatever you want."

Her eyes raked the powerful length of his body and she smiled. "What*ever* I want?"

He cleared his throat and cast a quick glance toward his boots.

"Why don't you take me to your bed?" she asked when he looked her way again.

He massaged his neck, looking as though she'd just put into words his greatest fantasy.

Temple retreated as he approached. She backed toward the staircase but he caught her before she made it halfway. Laughter filled the air as they headed to the second floor.

After a long night of lovemaking, Temple yearned for a full day of *more* lovemaking. She woke the next morning to find her husband dressing for work.

"No..."

"You stay right there." Mateo secured his belt and smiled at her through the dresser mirror. "That's where I want you when I get back, all right?"

Temple leaned back on her elbows. "Your tie." She giggled when he tossed a strip of rust-colored silk her way. Folding her legs beneath her, she draped the tie around his neck when he sat down on the bed. Instead of tying the material, she held it firmly and tugged him close.

"Stay home with me."

He let his forehead fall to her shoulder. "Baby, don't do this to me."

Intent on torturing her husband, Temple scooted closer until she was sitting astride him. "But I haven't done anything yet." The sheet was bunched about her waist, leaving her breasts bare. She nuzzled them into his shirt.

"Please," she murmured against his ear before suckling the lobe.

Mataeo clutched her bottom hidden within the folds of the sheet. "I should've married you a long time ago."

She smiled yet continued to suckle his earlobe. "I'm trying to give you a chance to make up for that."

"And I will. I promise." It was his turn to tend to *her* lobe. "Right after I handle this meeting."

Temple pulled back from him just a smidge. "A meeting?" She hoped she didn't sound too curious.

Mataeo didn't seem to notice. Grinding the muscle in his jaw, he set the sheet back in place across her chest. "Getting Yates's client list may've been the easy part. Now the work begins." He cupped her cheek and sent her a sly wink. "See you tonight?"

She stifled the many questions racing her mind and managed a nod.

Mataeo could understand the reason for his foul mood. All he could think of was Temple at home waiting for him—not a good train of thought when all it did was instill distinct discomfort below his waist.

Besides, there were matters more pressing just then. A meeting was called with all department heads to discuss Yates's former clientele. An extensive layout had been provided, detailing client preferences, products, vendors serviced, and so on. There was much work to be done to ensure a smooth transition of responsibilities from Yates World to North Shipping.

"Might I assume this monstrous workload is to blame for all these long faces?" Mataeo inquired.

Silence filled the room for several seconds and then a hand rose.

"Linc?"

Lincoln Brown nodded when Mataeo recognized him. "There've been some grumblings among a few of the clients—*our* clients not Yates's."

"What sort of grumblings?" Mataeo watched a few heads nod in agreement with Linc's announcement.

"They know about us acquiring the new list—the new dock station especially for them." Linc shrugged. "They're a little pissed that the new kids on the block are getting such special treatment."

"Christ." Mataeo rubbed a hand across his wide brow.

"That's not all." Dionne Spelling raised her hand while speaking. "There's an issue with that new dock—unforeseen…one of those things…but given the size of our barges and the square footage of the platform, it doesn't allow for the most efficient loading of our vessels."

All meeting attendees turned toward the youngest member of Ike Melvin's crew.

Dionne's smile relayed regret. "The dock is in a prime location, no doubt. Unfortunately, it lacks the adequate space needed to be as effective as our other locales."

"The location made it worth the purchase," Ike chimed in from his place in the chair closest to Mataeo's. "Only it may not work if we're planning to service these new folks exclusively from there and as efficiently as we do our other clients."

"Well, why can't we load on one side of the dock and handle paperwork from the other side?" someone suggested.

"Waste of time," Mataeo said.

"A widening project?"

"Waste of money." Mataeo shot down the second suggestion.

"Everybody, let's call it quits for the night, all right?" Ike said, sensing Mataeo's agitation. "We'll brainstorm some ideas, get together again…Mataeo?"

Mataeo gave consent with a slow nod.

"What I wouldn't give for Temple's brain at that meeting," Ike said once the group had dispersed. He grinned when Mataeo slanted him an ill-humored look. "Congratulations again," he drawled.

"Thanks." He gave a playful grimace then headed for the wall bar to prepare a stout glass of Jim Beam. "She doesn't need to be here. She got us the deal—it's up to us to make it work." He handed Ike a glass. "Besides, she's gone through enough working for me. She needs time away from all this." He considered his words while savoring the liquor when it hit his tongue.

"Understood." Ike downed the drink in one gulp. "However, would you be up for calling her if we don't find a solution good and quick?"

Mataeo grinned and approved Ike's suggestion by saluting him in a toast.

Smells of dinner in the air stopped Mataeo when he arrived that evening. For a while he just leaned against the front door and inhaled the aromas drifting out from the rarely used kitchen. Temple was cooking and, for the first time in all the years he'd lived there, the place felt like a home.

Mataeo pushed off the door, having caught sight of his wife leaving the dining room where she'd been setting the table. He caught up to her in the pantry—effectively blocking the doorway as she was making her way out.

Temple set the peaches back on the shelf as though they were an afterthought. "You're early," she breathed, going to her toes and brushing her mouth across his jaw.

Needing something more adequate, Mataeo cupped her chin, holding her in place for his kiss.

"What is it?" she asked when he'd loosened his embrace and she could see that his vibrant brown eyes were somewhat dimmed. "What's wrong?" She smoothed her thumb across his cheek.

Mataeo smothered a groan, wanting so much to confide, to seek her advice. To indulge in one of the millions of things he depended on her for.

"What's for dinner?" he asked instead, nuzzling his handsome face into the crook of her shoulder and taking refuge in her glorious scent.

"I was thinking about Claudia today."

"Aspen?" Mataeo chuckled while cutting into his third portion of the succulent smothered chicken breast that Temple had prepared. "What the hell for?"

"I was thinking of the client weekend we told her about, remember?"

He smiled and shook his head. "I honestly haven't thought about it since the day you came up with it."

"I thought now might be the perfect time to start planning something." Temple added more of the mixed vegetables to her plate. "With all our new clients, this might be a nice touch to reassure our loyal ones that we haven't forgotten about them."

Mateo leaned back in his chair at the head of the claw-foot, rectangular table. "Have you been to the office?"

"No. Why?"

He only shook his head.

Temple chewed thoughtfully on a stem of broccoli. "I just thought that since I've finally got the time, I'd like to plan something. Maybe here, if you don't mind." She kept her hazel stare on the ceramic plate. "There's definitely enough space."

"I don't want you overdoing anything, babe. God knows you've worked hard and long enough for me."

"Would you please stop with the self-pity?" She tossed her linen napkin his way. "It's not like I did it for free. And besides—" she toyed with the thin strap of the rose tank dress she wore "—I need something new to focus on."

Clenching a fist, Mateo once again forced himself to keep business matters stifled.

"Anyway." Temple pushed away her plate and gazed pointedly toward his. "Are you done? Because I'm very interested in going to bed."

The fork hit his plate with a clatter as he pushed back from the table and stood. In seconds it seemed, Mateo was swinging Temple into his arms and away they went.

* * *

Temple woke the next morning with intentions of making Mataeo breakfast. She found him already dressed and in the kitchen brooding over a cup of black coffee. She frowned, accepting that there was definitely something going on that he wouldn't or couldn't share with her.

She wasn't sure she wanted to know whatever it was, but they'd come too far to start keeping secrets. Biting the bullet, she cleared her throat and faced him with a bright smile when he turned.

"Can I ask you something?"

"Anything," he said after plying her with a second good-morning kiss.

She smiled sadly and tugged at the open collar of his shirt. "Do you think you made a mistake? With us, I mean?"

"What?" His gaze narrowed dangerously as his head dipped closer to hers.

Temple couldn't maintain eye contact. "It's just that we've been friends so long and I know it's an—an adjustment with—"

He set her atop the butcher-block countertop in one fluid move that effectively silenced her words.

"I'll only say this once more so listen to me good, all right?" He tangled a fist in her hair and tugged. "I love you. I always have and was too stupid to realize how much." He pressed his forehead to hers. "I know how much now and making you my wife was the best decision I ever made. Understood?"

She blinked, trying unsuccessfully to keep tears from flooding her eyes. "Understood."

* * *

"Is it that you just can't feel the daggers in your back or that you just don't give a damn about them anymore?"

Temple choked on laughter and the liquor she'd just taken a sip of when Megaleen asked her question.

"Both." She answered, bursting into laughter as Meg responded in kind. When the laughter waned, she came down a bit. "I'm so happy, Meg."

"And you have every right to be. The town's *still* buzzing about this. Men are envious of Mataeo while you've got *all* the ladies jealous."

"Then, all is well and nothing's changed except I'm so incredibly happy, Meg."

Meg leaned forward to squeeze both Temple's hands. "So why do I sense a 'but' about to make its way out?" She tapped her fingers on the rim of her glass and waited.

"I miss my job." Temple downed the remainder of her drink and signaled the waitress for another. "Don't get me wrong." She shook her head at Meg. "Having Mataeo was worth leaving for but…I wish I could've had both, you know?"

Meg shrugged beneath the cream sweater she wore. "So who says you can't?"

Temple was opening her mouth to respond when she changed her mind. "Give me a second, Meg." She left the table.

"Well, well, it's nice to see you dine amongst us little people every now and then."

Claudia Aspen turned and clasped her hands together when she saw Temple standing near. "Darlin'!"

She drew Temple into a double cheek kiss and hug. "It's nice to see that sexy husband of yours does let you out of bed every now and again." She took Temple's arm in a firmer grip then. "Now maybe I can get you to tell me what the hell you thought you were doing leavin' that way."

"Claudia? What? I—"

"I mean we were all hopin' you were just enjoying a little more of your honeymoon or vacation or whatever. Lord knows havin' a sweet thing like Mataeo North in your bed is enough to keep a woman exceptionally happy, but, sugar, it looks like you're in this for the long haul."

"Claudia…" Temple could see the strain clouding the woman's enhanced features. She urged her to take a seat at the table where a waiter stood dutifully to help Claudia into her chair.

"Now, what's really going on? What's got you so upset?"

"Well, let's see." In her typical dramatic fashion, Claudia gave an exaggerated eye roll and then fanned herself with one hand. "Besides, the fact that many of the local clients are in uproar—again."

"Uproar? Why?"

"Why, honey, folks do tend to get a mite jealous when they discover Yates and *his* clients are gettin' special first-class digs while the rest of us get our freight shipped through coach."

Temple closed her eyes then as it all fell into place. Mataeo's mood lately had to do with at least some of what Claudia was sharing. Still, Temple gave the woman the benefit of her attention and swore everything would be fine.

"How? Are you about to end this little extended vacation of yours?"

"Claudia…" Temple waited for the waiter to set down the coffee and ice water he'd arrived with. She waved off his request for her order. "It's not that simple," she said.

"Why? Has Mataeo fired you? Is he playing the 'husband who forbids his wife to work' role?"

"No, nothing like that. Only…"

Claudia frowned, clearly growing concerned. She tugged the cuff of the gold, silk wrap blouse Temple wore. "Tell me, darlin'."

"Claudia, I shouldn't have to tell you this. I mean you *are* tuned into all levels of the grapevine. You know what people think of my so-called working relationship with Mataeo."

"Why, darlin', whatever in the world are you talkin' about?"

"Claudia, please, half our clients probably think I 'assist' Mataeo more in his bedroom than in his office."

The woman blinked as if she'd been slapped. Understanding began to shimmer in her clear blue stare.

"I want to go back to work, but not back to that—to all that crap." Temple flopped back in the chair and muttered a more flagrant curse. "I don't know if you can understand this, Claudia. You run your own business—the head diva in charge. It's different when you work for the head diva and when he's sexy as sin."

"Honey." Claudia left her chair to select one closer to Temple at the wide round table. "Do you know how many times I've been accused of sleeping my way into a deal?" She shrugged. "I have to admit, though, that in my case it was often true." She joined in when Temple laughed.

"Listen." Claudia's expression grew stern. "A woman with a gorgeous boss and a load of innuendo can do two things. She can let petty women and wimpy men push her out of the game or she can play the game with all the skill and savvy she's mastered. Any woman who cuts down another for making it in this world is often-times a woman who's spent much of her time cutting out the beauty of being a woman for fear that it has no place in building a career in a *man's* world. And just so you know, the clients all adore you. They trust Mataeo even more so because they know he makes few moves without consulting you. He's a young icon in this busi-ness but still humble enough to seek outside counsel before making decisions—that says a lot about him."

"That hasn't made it any easier." Temple twisted the water glass, watching the ice clink against the sides. "I'd expect it from the outside, but I've taken crap from women who work right in the office."

Claudia waved a hand. "Some women see another who managed to keep her identity *and* craft a great career and they assume she's got an edge and that it in-volves working on her back, or on her knees, depend-ing…."

Temple burst into laughter.

Claudia smiled and squeezed her shoulder. "Have I made you feel better, darlin'?"

"Much."

"Enough for you to stop with this foolishness?"

Temple nodded. "Don't worry."

"I'll only do that if you tell me you're going back to work."

Temple decided on a slight change in topic. "Why don't you tell me whether you're coming to the client weekend? I haven't seen your RSVP yet."

Claudia sniffed. "Will you be making some sort of announcement there?"

Temple cast her hazel stare to the table and offered a minute shrug. "Guess you'll have to be there to find out."

"Well then." Playful wickedness crept back into Claudia's voice. "RSVP in the affirmative."

"Your husband won't mind about this, will he? I mean, we did date, after all."

"And it was one of the nicest half hours of my life." Temple began to laugh when Ike twirled her around as they danced.

The first annual client weekend for North Shipping's upper-tier clients was gearing up to be a rousing success. Every client RSVP'd in the affirmative, including former Yates World clientele. Mateo and Temple North's stunning beachfront spread proved to be the perfect locale for the event.

Temple had made a special effort to seek out Ike Melvin when he arrived. After her discussion with Claudia Aspen she made a beeline for the crew chief's office and didn't leave until he'd put her thoroughly back in the loop.

"So are you ready to do this?"

Temple began to nod. "Very ready. Thanks for telling me where things stood." She tugged his bow tie and smiled.

"Bonuses this year are apt to be pretty impressive. No way am I jeopardizing that. I knew you were the only one who could put us back on the right track."

"Thanks, Ike. Let's hope our boss agrees with you."

"Well, he's a fool if he doesn't and the man's no fool."

Temple scanned the crowded room. "Get everybody together and meet me in fifteen minutes."

Mataeo was last to arrive for the impromptu meeting called in his study. He found Temple leaning over his desk where she appeared to be studying a folder. He tugged at one of the tiny pearl buttons lining the back of the stylishly slinky ankle-length gown she wore.

"Baby." She favored him with an eager kiss and smile.

"What is this, Temp?"

"Have a seat." She ushered him behind the desk, ignoring the firm set to his magnificent features. "Everybody? I think we're ready to get this thing started."

Twenty minutes later, Temple had outlaid a solution to the debacle regarding the new dock. Her suggestion was so shockingly simple the hard-nosed execs were reluctant to admit their shame over not realizing it themselves.

Temple noted that the best route to take was to keep all North Shipping clients on equal footing. That meant all freight would be loaded in the same location. Seeing Yates's former clientele above North's tested and loyal customers would inevitably lead to a costly rift. The new dock would serve as a final stop before heading out into open waters. There, paperwork and any other last-minute matters would be handled. It went without saying that the group loved it. Everyone was full of cheers for Temple and excited about getting started on the new strategy. Mataeo appeared to be on board, as well, though he was noticeably quieter. While everyone else made their way back out to the party, he stayed seated behind his desk and watched his wife accept her accolades.

Uneasiness crept up Temple's spine with the departure of the last executive. She prepared herself with a deep breath before facing her husband.

"So?" she prompted, clasping her hands as she strolled toward the desk.

"So." Mataeo's sleek brows rose above his appealing stare while he shifted his chair to and fro.

"Pretty quiet," she noted.

He studied his hands and smirked. "You said it all, I guess."

"And you didn't say *anything* at all." She raised her chin when he suddenly looked her way. "Why didn't you tell me what was going on?"

"Because it's not your job anymore, or did you forget that?"

"Taeo, that doesn't mean I've lost interest in it or what happens to the company." She came around the desk to sit on the edge.

"You're my wife now." Stubbornly he set his fist beneath his jaw. "I don't want you having to deal with… whatever you'd have to deal with by being my wife *and* my…employee."

Temple couldn't help but chuckle. "Now it's *you* caring about what everyone else thinks."

"No." He rolled his eyes over the notion. "Hell, no. But you went through lots of pettiness around here. I'm sorry I was ever insensitive to that. I'm trying not to make that mistake again, Temp."

"I'll make you a deal." She curled her fingers around his lapel and urged him to stand before her. "If I can say 'to hell with what everyone thinks' then is it possible for you to stop trying to anticipate every little thing you think may or may not upset me?"

"That goes both ways, you know?" He sat next to her along the edge of the desk. "Forgive me for sounding like a chauvinist, but I sort of like the way you take care of me... I think you like it, too."

Temple fixed him with a phony surprised expression. "Do you expect me to believe that you know me as well as I know you?" She laughed when he shrugged.

"So have you got a solution for this one, too?" he challenged.

"Actually, I do." She dragged her knuckles across his jaw and enticed him into a brief kiss.

"Will you share?"

Temple nudged his shoulder. "Follow me."

"Everyone? Everyone, may I have your attention, please?"

Gradually, the crowd turned its attention toward the balcony where the host and hostess stood arm in arm.

"I want to thank all of you for attending this first client weekend. I hope this'll be the first of many."

Temple nuzzled back into Mataeo's strong form while the crowd cheered.

"I do have an announcement to make, so—"

"Mataeo, you scoundrel, already got the girl pregnant, eh?"

The newlyweds fell into laughter along with the rest of the group. Claudia Aspen's comment was well received but the couple quickly assured the guests that it wasn't true—yet.

Temple waved her hands to urge quiet again. "Seriously, everyone, this is about my work at North Shipping. I know many of you have wondered and I just want everyone to know that I plan to return in a few weeks but—"

Cheers and applause followed the announcement.

"*But* I won't be working myself silly." She nudged Mataeo's side. "Not at work, anyway."

"I'll have office hours three days a week and a few hours on Saturday," she announced once the next round of laughter silenced. "I think you guys need me almost as much as *this* guy." Temple's words were drowned out by applause when Mataeo turned her for a kiss.

"Is this okay?" she asked when they were hugging and his hands were smoothing the silk material of the dress where it covered her shoulders.

"It's very okay." Mataeo buried his face in her neck and inhaled deeply. "And I love you."

"I love you, too, but this isn't *exactly* the way you wanted it, though."

"I'm good and I love you."

"I hope so." Temple smiled when he repeated the

phrase and kissed her neck. "Looks like you're stuck with me for the duration."

Mataeo cupped her face. Any trace of playfulness was gone from his expression. Love and desire were all that remained. "And *that*," he said, "is exactly the way I want it."

* * * * *

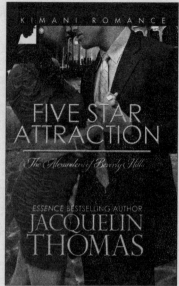

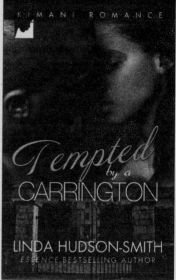

REQUEST YOUR FREE BOOKS!

2 FREE NOVELS PLUS 2 FREE GIFTS!

KIMANI™
ROMANCE

Love's ultimate destination!